Wedding a WARRIOR

A Novella

by

Hannah Conway

Published by

Olivia Kimbrell Press™

Olivia Kimbrell Press ™

Wedding a Warrior, a Novella

PUBLISHED BY: Olivia Kimbrell Press™*, P.O. Box 4393, Winchester, KY 40392-4393.

The Olivia Kimbrell Press™ colophon and open book logo are trademarks of Olivia Kimbrell Press™.

*Olivia Kimbrell Press™ is a publisher offering true to life, meaningful fiction from a Christian worldview intended to uplift the heart and engage the mind.

Some scripture quotations courtesy of the King James Version of the Holy Bible.

Some scripture quotations courtesy of the New King James Version of the Holy Bible, Copyright© 1979, 1980, 1982 by Thomas-Nelson, Inc. Used by permission. All rights reserved.

Library Cataloging Data
U.S. Library of Congress Control Number (PCN): 2015930106
Conway, Hannah (Hannah Conway) 1983-
 Wedding a Warrior / Hannah Conway
 142 p. 20cm x 12.5cm (8in x 5in.)
Summary: Whitleigh wrestles with faith and ponders how to answer longtime boyfriend, Collier, now Army soldier, who unexpectedly proposes. Marriage would mean leaving behind everything she's ever known, loved, and planned for in life.
 ISBN-13: 978-1-939603-64-7 (CreateSpace)
 ISBN-10: 1-939603-64-1
1. Christian fiction 2. man-woman relationships 3. military romance 4. love stories 5. family relationships 6. Christian romance
PS3568.H623 0113 2015
[Fic.] 813.6 (DDC 23)

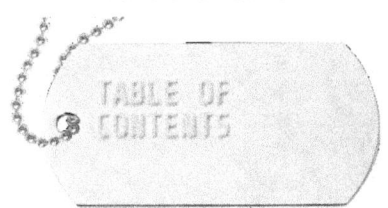

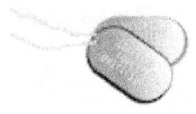

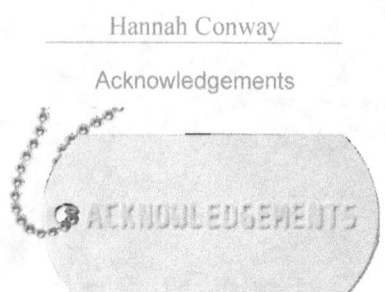

ACKNOWLEDGEMENTS

I want to thank God. I pray these words reflect who He is and nothing that I've done of my own accord.

I want to thank my husband for his service to our country and family. You keep me steady.

To my babies, I love you both and your sweet hugs. You are a joy.

To my family back home in Kentucky, I thank you for your unending encouragement.

To ACFW, MBT, and all my writer friends for your encouragement, guidance, and instruction in priceless.

A big thank you to my publishers, Olivia Kimbrell Press. Heather McCurdy, my amazing editor, and Debi Warford, my talented cover artist, thank you.

I want to acknowledge and thank my readers and influencers. Your support brings a smile to my face and it's a privilege to pray for you. You are vital to my writing ministry.

To all my friends who stand by my side, I love doing life with you. Thank you for your encouragement.

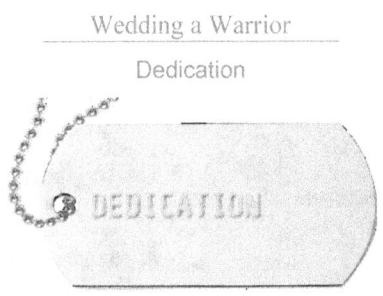

This book is dedicated to my mom and dad.

Psalm 127:4

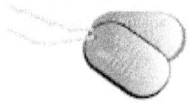

YES, they'd have at least twelve children. Minimum. Whitleigh Haynes held Collier Cromwell's note in one hand. An elbow weighted down a short stack of Kindergarten artwork and handwriting papers ready to be graded. She sat cross-legged at the playground picnic table and held her chin in the palm of her other hand. Her eyes scanned the Kentucky sky far more blue than yesterday.

The clouds looked lovely today—puffy. Whitleigh squinted and lifted a hand above her brow as a shield from the sun's bright rays. She breathed in the sweet scent of freshly mowed grass and hints of early autumn leaves. Cars hummed by in the distance.

Fibers from her cardigan sleeve tickled her nose. She laughed almost as loud as the children running around. Both kindergarten classes competed in a clumsy game of tag. A swift breeze played along, tossing strands of their hair up and about. It lifted her hair as well, throwing it over one shoulder. Whitleigh slid the bobby pin back into place just above her ear.

Back to work—if she could concentrate. Mrs. Ruthers needed as much help as possible getting papers graded and sent out to parents before the weekend. If Whitleigh were to have a classroom of her own one day, she needed all the practice she could get.

Collier interfered with her thought process way too often. Not a bad problem.

She clicked her short nails on the table and slid his letter in a bulging tote bag. Glue sticks, stickers, and crayons bumped against lip gloss, her college and life planner, order forms for painted frames, and that horrid barbeque-stained apron rolled up and ready to wear for another evening of work.

Whitleigh dug around in the tote, pushing her cell phone and car keys to the side. Volunteering at the school meant no pay, but waitressing and customizing old picture frames provided enough to supply the kiddos in Mrs. Ruthers' class with an assortment of stickers and sweet treats. She smiled and lifted a stack of stickers thicker than the papers needing to be graded.

The first paper, letter recognition and association—Abi. Whitleigh brushed over the little girl's name with her thumb and smiled.

Frail pencil lines struggled to follow along the dotted path of the F. Much improved from last time. Whitleigh placed a glitter-clad sticker on the child's rendition of the American flag and drew a smile beside each letter attempt on the paper. She licked her fingers, nodded, tucked the page behind the next, and moved on. Fantastic work.

"Ms. Haynes. Ms. Haynes." A group of rambunctious, lose toothed kiddos shouted in her direction. "Come play with us."

"Ha." Whitleigh threw back her head. "In these shoes?"

"You can take'm off."

Teachers and staff walked up and down the sidewalk nearest to the playground, many looking like wardens, while others frolicked alongside the children.

"Coming." Whitleigh's cheeks hurt from smiling. Yes, one day she and Collier would have many children, and she'd have a classroom of children just like the ones she helped now. Whitleigh stood from the child-sized table and slipped off her high-heeled shoes. She glanced at the note from Collier once more. Sigh. The man was a poet. Her fingers danced along the last line.

"It's a good thing there's an eternity. A lifetime with you isn't enough. Looking forward to our date today. I have something important to ask."

Her cheeks warmed. A proposal neared. She knew it. Reese and Lennon saw him looking at rings with his buddies at the mall the other day. Whitleigh giggled and her heart quickened. Of course she'd say yes.

Mrs. Whitleigh Cromwell. Nice. Her mouth slid into a grin.

Had he asked Dad for permission? Surely. Collier was thorough.

"Hurry up." The children arched their backs, arms extended as they exaggerated their plea.

Whitleigh threw a teasing nod in their direction. "Okay. Okay." She folded the letter and slid it beneath the note pages of her clipboard. "You guys think you can outrun me?"

Their small squeals resembled the brakes of her poor car, but much more entertaining and free. They bounced up and down without the assistance of caffeine. "Come get us."

Whitleigh bumped her hip as she rounded the corner of the table and rubbed the spot as if it helped the pain.

"I'm it now." Whitleigh held her up hands, fingers curled. "You better run. Here I come."

The children scattered. Their mouths opened wide and released quirky cackles. They paid no mind to the disapproving nods of older teachers and faculty members propped against the chain-link fence. Each child darted to and fro, many of their shoe strings flapping along the grass. Whitleigh chased them around the swings, through the sandbox, and past the double slides. Her breaths escaped in heaps of laughter.

"Whew. Y'all are too fast for me." Whitleigh gasped for air. Her fists rested on her hips. The children giggled as they ran toward her. Her open arms hugged as many of them as possible.

"Blood." Landry's eyes widened as she pointed. Her tiny mouth formed a perfect oval. She tugged on her red pigtails. "Brady's bleeding again."

Poor guy. Fourth time this month. Whitleigh pried tiny hands from her neck and tickled her way through the mob of grumbling five and six year-olds.

"Brady always gets hurt." Jameson stuck out his bottom lip, arms folded. "We were having fun until you got hurt, Bra-dy."

Brady hid his face behind his knees.

"Be nice, Jameson." Whitleigh rustled his unruly brown hair as she worked her way past the children and knelt to the ground. "Another skinned knee." She scooped Brady in her arms. "It's a good thing you've only got two knees kiddo." He didn't snicker.

Brady buried his head into Whitleigh's shoulder.

"Okay kiddos." Whitleigh strained as she lifted Brady. Stout little boy. "Keep playing. You've still got a few minutes of recess left until Mrs. Ruthers comes to get you."

They groaned and kicked at the ground, but then ran off, bent on enjoying the remainder of recess.

"I'm still watching, so be nice to each other."

Jameson crinkled his nose before starting off toward the sandbox.

Brady's sobs were short and quiet for the most part. "I tore my new jeans." He sniffled. "My mom and dad are gonna be so mad." Tears fell from his hazel eyes.

Whitleigh's throat tightened. "Shh." She held him close and carried him over to the picnic table. "Don't worry about that." But he would. Kids in this area of Kentucky knew from a young age how hard parents worked to provide for their families. "You sit right here." She placed him on top of the table and hollered toward the fence row. "Mrs. Jefferies. First aid kit, please."

Mrs. Jefferies, another teacher's aide, much older than she, hurried toward the school hands up as she ran.

Brady held his knee and panted. Whitleigh sat at his side. "Mrs. Jefferies is on her way." She wrapped an arm around him. "How about we talk about something. Anything you want." That should keep his mind off the wound. "Toys. Pizza. Superheroes. You name it." Whitleigh wiped the tears from his cheek with the sleeve of her cardigan.

"Did you know our country is in a war?"

"Um." Whitleigh winced. "Yes. I did know that." The attacks of September 11th left the world in turmoil. "You want to tell me about your latest Lego creation?"

Brady shook his head. "My Dad is going to the war. He holunteered."

"Volunteered?"

"Yeah. He leaves on Monday."

"That's really brave of your father."

"He's braver than superman." Brady lifted his chin, chest puffed out.

"Yes, he is." Whitleigh tousled his blond hair. Her eyes brimmed with tears. Much like Brady she fought them back.

"Momma cries." Brady swiped his arm across his nose. "She doesn't know I hear her. I think she's scared for Daddy to go."

Perceptive child.

Whitleigh's chest caved. Her stomach lurched. "It's hard to let go of someone you love." What did she, a young college student, know about letting go when all she'd done was hold on? Home was here, in a safe place, with her family close by and

Collier at her side—together forever. "Your mom is brave too you know."

Brady's brow furrowed.

"She is." Whitleigh pulled him closer. "Believe it or not."

The whistle blew. Mrs. Ruthers waved to her class. "Time to go."

The children protested in unison, but skipped forward, making a rather lengthy and crooked line.

Mrs. Jefferies scuttled from the side doors of the school with an assortment of first aid items. One bandage would've sufficed.

Whitleigh patted Brady's leg. "Your daddy is going to be okay and so is your mommy." Why make such a promise when nothing in life was guaranteed? Whitleigh lowered her lashes.

"Will you pray for them Ms. Haynes?"

Her eyes stung. Precious child. "Of course."

"My grandpa told me God makes all things work out good for those who love Him."

"Your grandpa is a smart man."

"I love God."

"Me too buddy."

He poked at the frayed pieces of denim around his skinned knee as if contemplating to speak, or perhaps he tried to grasp the concept of all things working for the good of those who love God. A daunting task, yet, if anyone could comprehend the mind of God, it would be a child.

Mrs. Jefferies came closer. She fumbled with the bandage wrappers, cotton swabs, and antibiotic ointment. Brady winced as she busied herself dabbing, prodding, and wrapping his wound. "All better." Her wrinkled rounded cheeks jiggled as she nodded her head.

Brady smiled, his tears now dried. He hugged Mrs. Jefferies and she hurried about working to straighten the line of Kindergarteners. Mission impossible.

"It's a good thing I got hurt, Ms. Haynes."

Whitleigh tilted her head. "Good?"

"If I didn't get hurt, then I wouldn't have been able to ask you to pray for my Mom and Dad before he left."

Profound. A short breath escaped her mouth. Tingling shivers spread up her back. She welcomed the tiny arms around her neck and rocked Brady side to side for a moment.

"This was my only time to ask." He shrugged, breaking from the hug. "We can't really talk in class."

"You've got a point." Whitleigh snickered and nodded. Mrs. Ruthers liked a quiet classroom.

Another whistle blew and the children marched and hopped into the elementary school.

"C'mon kiddo, I'll walk you to class." Whitleigh slid from the picnic tabletop holding Brady's small hand in hers.

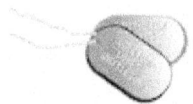

SO this was where Collier would propose. Wildflowers basked in the glow of the sun's rays. To her right and left tall oaks, maples, poplars, and ash trees lifted their branches to dance in the wind. Their leaves clattered together like applause. Perhaps they could cheer louder when Collier decided to take a knee. Whitleigh smiled and laid her head on his shoulder as they walked along the familiar, narrow dirt path.

She carried her high-heels in one hand and held Collier's hand with the other. The wicker picnic basket creaked in the crook of his elbow. A rolled up quilt peeked from beneath the basket lid.

"You're more quiet than usual." Collier gave her hand a slight squeeze. "Still thinking of Brady?"

"Among other things." Whitleigh's grin slid to the side. She lifted her head and kicked a rock to the side. "He's so brave. His dad leaves in a couple of days and instead of whining about how unfair life is, he's asking me to pray for his parents."

Collier nodded.

"That child has more faith than I have."

"How so?" Collier tilted his head.

"I've never left the comfort of my own home, nor do I really even want to."

"What about the mission trip to Honduras next summer?"

Yeah. What about it? Whitleigh shrugged. "I'll go, it's just... I can't explain it." She huffed. "I know I'm supposed to do missions, but I don't know if this is the one. Know what I mean?" She tilted her head.

"So...."

"I'll go to Honduras, but I feel like there's something more for me out there, you know?"

"Something bigger than a trip to Honduras?"

Whitleigh nodded. Her heart quickened. "A life calling." She closed her eyes for a moment. "Teaching, loving, helping, serving." She sucked in a sharp breath. "It's like there's something in me that I have to do or I'm going to explode." A laugh escaped from her mouth.

"I know all about that." Collier swallowed with an audible gulp.

"Tell me what you know about, Mr. Cromwell." Whitleigh spun on the balls of her feet under his arm as if on a ballroom floor instead of the leaf strewn ground.

"You first." Collier twirled her around a second time, careful to balance the picnic basket. "I wanna hear about this 'life calling' and how you're gonna keep from exploding. Wouldn't want that to happen."

"Ha. Well." Whitleigh lowered her chin as she matched his steps with her short stride. "I get glimpses of what I'm supposed to do, but I'm not sure how it all plays out." She licked her lips. "I love kids. Becoming a teacher is a good place to start. Then one day there will be marriage, babies, and summer missions." She nudged his shoulder.

"Is that all?"

"Isn't it enough?" She stopped and pulled him back as he continued ahead.

"Maybe for now." Collier winked. His words lingered in her heart. She winced and hurried back to his side.

"Anyway." The dirt floor felt cool beneath her feet. "Brady's embarking on this life journey that I could never go on." She shook her head. "He's facing so many unknowns." Whitleigh shivered.

Collier lifted her hand to his mouth and then let their hands hang down to dangle side to side. Her fist bumped his hip and brushed against his blue jeans. No ring box in that pocket.

Whitleigh arched a brow. "You plan on telling me that thing you have to do or you're gonna explode?"

"Looking for the right time."

Her face warmed. She couldn't help but giggle. Collier looked up. Whitleigh followed his gaze. Beautiful clouds peeked between the canopies of tree branches.

Whitleigh watched as a squirrel scurried up a tree. Tall grasses clung close to the tree trunks and bent forward to tickle her ankles.

"You love those kids." Collier stepped over a tree branch lying along the path.

"I'm glad it's obvious." She intertwined her fingers with his—where they belonged. "They may be five and six years old, but those kids are strong and good to the core."

"Jameson too?"

"Ha." Whitleigh threw her head back. "Jameson too."

"He put glue in a little girl's hair."

"Lilly said she wanted her hair to sparkle." Whitleigh giggled and swung her arm out to the side, dodging another fallen limb on the ground. "Jameson was helping the glitter stay."

"Our kids will be just as mischievous."

Our kids. Whitleigh's lungs filled with air, but it sure seemed more like delight. She pressed her lips together and fought the burning in her cheeks.

Collier cleared his throat. He must be nervous about proposing.

"Whit." He stopped and turned to face her. Her shoes fell from her hand and onto the ground. They could stay there. "I know you think you're not brave and strong, but you are." His eyes, pools of blue, invited her to dive in. Could this be the proposal? She formed her lips to speak, but perhaps he had more to say. "Day in and day out you're at the school volunteering to help all of those kids."

"Most come from poor fam—"

"You work double shifts waitressing, and refurbishing old stuff to sell."

"Got to make a living." Whitleigh blew a piece of hair from her face. "And I want to go on the mission trip to Honduras next summer—though leaving here kind of terrifies me."

Collier held a finger over her mouth and smiled.

Whitleigh twisted her lips to the side, lowering her eyes from his. If she didn't keep quiet, she would ruin her own proposal. Her gal pals, Reese and Lennon would flip.

"You don't see how wonderful you are. How special." He lifted her chin with a finger. His lips fit perfectly against hers. Whitleigh's body weakened as she sighed.

A brash upturned wind swept through the woods. Leaves swirled around them. The moment as nearly magical.

The breeze settled, but her heartbeat did not. Whitleigh kept her eyes closed.

"Now that's a kiss." Collier brushed a leaf from her hair and placed one more kiss on her cheek. "Even Mother Nature agrees."

"You had something you wanted to ask me, right?" She tucked her bottom lip beneath her front teeth. "The letter said, um." Stop talking. Whitleigh licked her lips as her stomach worked itself into knots. The anxiety was too much to handle.

"A little further and we'll talk. Promise."

Whitleigh knit her brows together, but followed at his side. She stepped over stones and divots. The woods were alive and overflowing with proof of God's creative genius. Her eyes scanned the vastness of her surroundings, but could not process all of the details. Collier picked the most incredible setting to ask for her hand in marriage. Her cheeks lifted. Who should she call first? Mom and Dad? Reese and Lennon?

"Beautiful, huh?"

"I love the woods." Whitleigh squeezed his hand. She closed her eyes, breathing in the earthy scent.

Collier coughed. His palms dampened.

"How about here?"

"Huh?"

"For our picnic." Collier stopped and nodded to a clearing in the woods off to the right.

"Oh." Picnic. Focus Whitleigh.

Collier placed the wicker basket on the ground. Twigs crunched beneath its weight. He shook out the quilt and spread it on the ground.

Trees in the early stages of their autumn transformation created a pleasant awning. "It's beautiful."

Collier sat on the edge of the patchwork quilt and extended a hand. Whitleigh reached out to join him.

"Your life calling." He propped himself up with one arm. "Am I a part of it?"

Didn't he already know? Her throat tightened. "The most certain part."

He nodded, bowing his head as if to hide a grin. Collier took her hands in his. They warmed at his touch. "You're a part of my life calling too, Whit, but…." he trailed off as he looked away.

"But?" Her eyes searched his face.

"There's another part. A part I've been fighting for some time."

Whitleigh crossed her legs and leaned forward. What wasn't he telling her?

"I know you don't believe you're as brave as Brady, but I think you are."

"What are you getting at Collier?"

"You want to be with me, and I want to be with you."

"Of course."

"Even if we face unknowns, possibly the same uncertainties as Brady and his family?"

"I don't understand."

Collier sighed. He tucked his chin and then lifted his head. His blue eyes watered. "Whit, I'm joining the Army."

Whitleigh's hand shot over her mouth. She worked to

breathe. Her trembling fingers broke free from his embrace. How could Collier do such a thing?

Her tears ran faster than what her feet could take her. Away. She needed to get away from him as quickly as possible. Whitleigh ran and held her arms tight across her chest. Falling apart could wait. She ignored Collier as he called out. The dorms, blurred through her teary vision, came into sight over the hill. Her feet patted against the ground. A few more strides and she'd be in the safety of her room, able to lock out the man who threatened to crush her dreams.

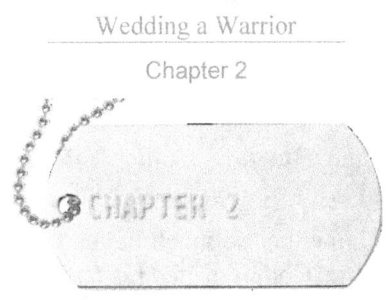

CHAPTER 2

"I don't know what went wrong." Collier wrung his hands over his face. He dialed Whit's number. It rang. No answer. He tossed the cellphone on the beat up beanbag and growled. "One minute she's saying she wants to be with me and the next she's running away crying."

"Women." Bryant coughed into his fist. Collier threw darts with his eyes. Bryant lowered his head.

"You should've proposed first, man." Blaine sat on the edge of the bed, elbows resting on his knees.

"I'm pretty sure she wouldn't appreciate that." Collier shook his head. "Thanks for marrying me Whit, oh, and by the way, I'm joining the Army."

Blaine laid back on the bed. "Point taken."

"Besides, now's not the right time to go asking her to marry me." *Right?* Collier drew in a long breath and raked a hand through his hair.

Bryant didn't have much to say, other than his snide comment. He and Blaine, though twins, couldn't be more different. Bryant sat nestled down in an old orange lounge chair in the corner of their dorm. His smug stare caused Collier's eyes to narrow. No matter how often Bryant denied it, his silence proved he still had feelings for Whit.

"I bet you're loving this." Collier's words bit more than intended.

"Don't drag me into this, Collier." Bryant held out open palms. "I told you Whit wouldn't go for it."

"'Cause you know her so much better, right?" Those words were intended to bite. Collier gritted his teeth.

"We grew up together. What do you think?" Lines appeared across Bryant's forehead as his tone deepened.

"I've grown up with her too." Collier stepped toward Bryant. Bryant rose from the lounge chair.

"C'mon guys. We're all friends here." Blaine placed a palm on their shoulders.

"Roommates don't have to be friends." Bryant's nostrils flared.

Collier didn't back down. "I can live with that."

"Guys. For real?" Blaine pushed between them. "We've always been friends. Don't do this over a girl."

"A girl?" Bryant shoved his brother to the side. Blaine frowned, dusted off his plaid button up shirt, and rolled his eyes. "Whit's not just any girl."

Collier tightened his bottom lip, fist ready to fly.

Bryant folded his arms and arched his back. "Whit's a small-town girl. Simple. Sweet. She wants a calm life with security."

"And what, Bryant?" Collier narrowed his eyes. "You're the one to give her that life? You're gonna be in the Army, too, in a couple of years."

"That's right. I will be." Bryant tightened his jaw. "And you'll be saluting me."

Ouch. Collier swallowed.

"Bryant, dude." Blaine pushed his brother back. "Dad would go nuts if he heard you talking like that. Officer or not, we will respect all ranks."

Bryant lowered his head.

Collier's stomach twisted. He stood down and relaxed his stance. "Bryant, man, I'm sorry." He ran a hand over the back of his head. "I shouldn't be taking all this out on you."

"Whit loves you, Collier." Bryant's eyes glanced to the side. He slid his hands into the pocket of his hooded sweatshirt. "I know she loves you." He shifted his stance and shrugged. "She and I had our chance and it didn't work out."

The two stared at one another for a solid minute. Could Bryant be trusted? He only had Whit's best interest in mind.

Collier nodded and extended a hand. "Friends?"

Bryant's shook it with a firm grip. "Friends."

"See." Blaine nodded and gave his hands a quick clap. "It's all good."

Their hands fell to their sides in silent secession.

Collier sighed. "I don't want to lose her." He bit at his thumbnail. "I don't know how to make this right. I mean," he huffed, "I've prayed about this."

"Prayed about joining the Army?" Blaine's brows lifted.

"Of course. Haven't you? I'm supposed to go."

Blaine offered a half shrug and sat back down on the bottom bunk.

Bryant leaned against the concrete wall of their dorm room, arms folded across his chest. "And what about marrying her? You prayed about that?"

"What other reason did I have for dragging you guys to a jewelry store?" Collier bit at the inside of his lip. "I know she and I are supposed to be together."

Bryant sighed, his mouth turned down.

"So what's the holdup?" Blaine's face folded. Geez, he and Bryant looked way too much alike with those crazy green eyes. Spooky. "They were having great sales on engagement rings. You should've taken advantage of those."

Collier squinted and Bryant shook his head, lips pressed into a thin line.

"What?" Blaine lifted his shoulders.

"I worry about you sometimes." Bryant planted a punch into his twin's shoulder.

Collier cracked a smile. "Well." He scratched at his cheek. Hints of stubble scraped beneath his fingers. "I'm not sure what the holdup is. I guess I'm waiting for the right time. Right conditions, you know?"

Bryant scoffed. "And what are those?"

Collier pinched the bridge of his nose. "Maybe when she graduates in two years? I'll be stable by then. You know, able to provide a better life for her." The kind of life he never had. The kind of life she deserved.

"You think she'll wait that long for you?" Bryant's tone carried hints of hope in his own favor.

Collier flinched as if the words smacked him across the face. Would she wait?

"It's a legitimate question." Blaine nodded and rested a closed hand on his chin.

"You better figure it out soon, Collier." Bryant lifted his chin higher. "Whit's a good girl and I'd hate to see her hurt." He pulled the hood of his hoodie over his head. "C'mon Blaine, there's a million other things we could be doing right now."

Collier stood near the large open dorm window, his back

away from the door. It shut with a thud. The sound echoed through the room.

He leaned against the window sill and lifted his eyes. "What do I do now?"

A prayer was a prayer, even if sent up as a question.

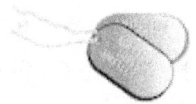

COLLIER rocked back on the heels of his shoes and shoved his hands into his coat pocket. If Whit wouldn't answer his calls, then maybe she'd wait his table.

The bells on the door jingled as he entered the barbecue joint. A wave of warmth swirled around his face from the raging fireplace. He held his hands toward the heat and the chill from the September night air melted away.

He scanned the small space. Concrete floors. Booths made with barn wood and dressed in red and white gingham. Metal cutouts of happy pigs holding BBQ sauce hung on the barn wood walls. Doubt the pigs in that place were too happy. Collier smiled at his joke and cleared his throat. For a Friday night, The Feeding Trawf looked unusually empty. A few families chatted over their meal and a couple of older men sucked on root beers at the bar. He strained his neck, looking around the corner of the fireplace. No Whit.

"Can I help you?" Reese snarled at him from the hostess stand. Collier's face warmed. What did Reese know about anything anyway? Not the whole story, that's for sure.

"You make me feel so welcome."

"Then I'm not doing my job well."

"C'mon Reese." Collier's chest rose and fell. "Can you put me in Whit's section?"

"I'm sure you'd rather Lennon serve you tonight."

"She probably hates me right now too."

"Who doesn't?" Reese squinted as her voice rose a few octaves. "But she's less likely to poison your food than Whit."

Nice. Collier nodded and twisted his mouth to the side.

"Good thing I'm not too hungry tonight."

Reese grumbled as she grabbed a menu.

Whit pushed through the kitchen swinging doors near the back of the restaurant. With an arm in the air, she balanced a large round tray on one hand. A few strands of hair hung loose around her face, falling from her ponytail. Beautiful.

She smiled at the folks sitting in one of her section booths and placed their food in front of each of them. A little boy thanked her and she patted him on the head, handing him an extra set of crayons with an "our little secret" wink.

That woman…

"Pick your jaw up and stop drooling." Reese's eyebrow nearly touched her hairline. "C'mon Romeo. Don't say I didn't warn you."

Collier slid into a corner booth. For now, Whit hadn't seen him. Andy, the night manager passed by.

"What's up Collier?" He gave a high five. "Always good to see you."

Collier returned the five with a smile. "You know Trawf is spelled wrong?"

"So you keep telling me." Andy smacked Collier's shoulder and carried on as usual. "The owner thinks it's a clever play on words."

"So you keep telling me." Collier shook his head.

"Oops." Lennon came from nowhere, falling forward with

drinks in her hand.

Collier had no place to go. He lunged forward, knocking over the booth table. Barbecue bottles flew in the air. Soda drenched his pants. Ice cubes fell to the concrete floor as Collier jumped from his seat and reached for the glass bottles. He missed and they crashed onto the floor, splattering an impressive amount of sauce into many different directions.

After a few gasps The Feeding Trawf fell silent. Lennon stood, wide eyed, with both hands hovering over her mouth. Three shades of barbecue speckled Andy's body. Collier stood, carbonated pants and all. He grabbed napkins scattered about the floor and wiped off his arms. The vinegar smell remained. Whit saw that. The whole place saw that.

She stared at him, mouth closed, eyes filled with words... questions.

Collier shrugged.

"I'm so sorry Collier." Lennon dabbed at the stains on his fleece jacket with the end of her apron. "I didn't mean to, I mean—"

"You mean you didn't think accidentally spilling drinks on me would turn into this big of a mess?" Collier frowned.

"Something like that." Lennon's cheeks matched the darker shade of barbecue sauce decorating the floor.

"I'm okay, Andy." Collier threw up a short wave.

Andy nodded and hurried back with a mop and bucket. He peered over his thick glasses at Lennon. "I think you know how to use this."

She huffed, but grabbed the mop and got busy.

Andy pointed to Whit. "Take fifteen. I got your tables covered."

She nodded, untied her apron, slipped it over her head, and passed by Collier without even looking in his direction. Collier's shoulders fell. Maybe coming here wouldn't help.

He followed her into the kitchen, past the broilers and ovens, and into a break room the size of a closet. Whit scooted a metal chair from beneath a beat-up card table, and sat. He missed her smile, even the one meant for customers.

"Can we talk?" Collier inched toward her and eased into the creaking chair across from her.

"I didn't mean to run away like that today." Her lashes skimmed the tops of her cheeks. She lifted her eyes. "I didn't know what else to do." She held her arms as if cradling herself. Collier moved a hand toward her, but then pulled back. Now wasn't the time to hold her. Now was the time to listen.

"Were you, um, are you, we are okay, right?" His voice tripped over his thoughts. Collier licked his lips.

Whit's chin dropped to her neck. Not a good sign. Collier held his breath.

"I'm sorry about what Lennon did to you." Her voice sounded above a whisper.

"This?" Collier licked the remnants of sauce from his thumb and squeezed soda from his pant leg. He forced a laugh. "Nah. I've had worse. She's just being a good friend."

A smirk grew across Whit's face. Collier's chest rose. He smiled back and reached for her hand. She didn't pull away and he cradled her palms between his.

"Whit, I didn't mean to hurt you." He brushed her wrists with both thumbs. "Springing news like that on you must've been hard to hear."

She sat back and released a sigh too heavy for his liking. "I thought you were going to propose."

"What?" Collier's throat constricted. "What gave you that idea?" He worked to swallow and almost missed her wince.

Her lashes fluttered faster than the red reaching her cheeks.

"Lennon and Reese saw you at the mall."

"Oh." He leaned forward, touching their hands to his forehead. "I'm the one who should be sorry."

"So you weren't looking at rings?"

"I was." He raised his head and met her eyes.

"You do want to marry me?"

"Yes. One day."

"And you're really leaving for the Army?"

"I have to."

"Because you feel it's what God wants you to do?"

"Because I know He wants me to."

"Those people out there. The table I was waiting on when, well," she pointed to the soda and barbecue on his clothes. "That's Brady and his family. The little boy from school whose dad deploys on Monday." Her eyes watered. "He wanted to bring his mom and dad to meet me." She sniffled. "They thanked me for praying for them."

"I'll be okay, Whit."

"You don't know that." She yanked a hand away and swiped at a tear.

No, he couldn't promise his safety or the well-being of Brady's father.

"You leaving—joining the Army." She shook her head and tucked her lip under her teeth. "It's a lot to process."

"I have every intention of coming back for you." Collier gave her hands a squeeze. "Please wait for me. Two years."

"After graduation?"

"That gives me time to prepare a good life for us. You'll graduate and land a teaching job. Sky's the limit for us."

"Is the Army a career or—"

"I honestly don't know." His shoulders skimmed the bottom of his ears. "I can tell you that as of right now, it's only going to be three years."

"And then done?"

"Done." He couldn't promise an uncertainty. "That's the plan at least." Collier blinked. He brought her hand to his lips. "Three years will fly. Two of those years you'll be so busy with school and work you won't even miss me."

Whitleigh sniffled through a smile. "How will I get through Professor Rhine's class without you next semester?"

"Bryant always keeps it interesting." What an understatement. "I'm sure you'll manage."

"When do you leave?" Her long lashes lowered and then rose.

"I'm going to swear in next week, but I won't have to leave until early next semester. Delayed entry program." Collier intertwined his fingers with hers. Her hand appeared small in comparison with his. "I needed to finish out the semester. Finish well and spend as much time as possible with you."

Collier leaned forward. He kept hold of her hands as she squirmed about in her chair, head lowered. Whit ran from anything out of her comfort zone. Who wouldn't? She closed her eyes as if it helped clear her mind. Her inner struggle marked an outward expression with each twisted grimace.

"I know you're scared, Whit." He lifted her hands to his lips. "If you had no fear, no setbacks, what would your answer be?"

"It's not that easy." She shook her head and sucked in a deep breath. "You know what I'd say if it were that simple."

"Have faith, Whit."

Whitleigh rolled her eyes. "This isn't how things were

supposed to go for us."

"Don't you think I know this?" Collier scooted from the table. The chair screeched against the concrete floor. Whit could be so stubborn. Where was her faith? "Plans change and we can trust God even if His plans look different from what we have in mind."

He reached for Whit's hand. She stood from the table and faced him. Her blue eyes gazed up at him and pierced his heart. How could someone so pure, so kind, and lovely have so much reluctance? Collier swallowed.

"Whit." He kissed her forehead. "Just wait for me, that's all I'm asking. Please."

She wrapped her arms around his neck. For being petite that girl had a grip. Her expression grew resolute. "I will wait for you. As long as it takes."

Collier opened his mouth to speak, but she pulled him close, placing her lips on his. Where did that thought go? Whatever he had to say could wait.

"Ahem. Knock, knock."

Collier pried Whit's arms from around his neck. "I'm sorry, Sir."

Andy laughed. The dim light overhead gave his aged skin a yellow hue. "Break's over."

Whit covered a sweet smile with her hand. "See ya after work." She scooted past Collier. The tips of their fingers prolonged the goodbye.

Collier sighed. She said she'd wait. His back pressed against the barn wood wall. Life was good.

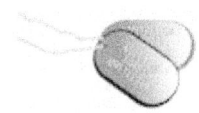

CHAPTER 3

WHITLEIGH crossed her arms around a set of binders and books, pressing them firmly against her chest. Her shoulders protested, laboring beneath the straps of her cumbersome backpack. If only time remained for a quick stop at the dorm. Rain drizzled from the gray clouds above, a sure sign that spring had arrived in Kentucky. She tucked her head until the tip of her nose touched the *Basics of Education and European History* textbooks. Regardless of her attempts to avoid the drops, the rain continued to beat a steady rhythm on top of her head. Whitleigh batted a raindrop from her lashes, or maybe a tear. Those came without warning lately, ever since Collier left. Where had their time together gone?

The clock tower chimed and resonated throughout the campus. Class started in five. Her sneakers picked up the pace, racing faster than the dribbles of sweat spiraling down her back from kickboxing — an easy but much needed stress reducing elective. She wove through the morning coffee shop line pouring out onto the sidewalk. Fragrant bold blends awakened her senses. Her feet rounded the neatly landscaped corner.

Oh great. The pickles.

Whitleigh kept her head lowered, passing the college cadets in their Army green ROTC uniforms, huddled on picnic tables beneath the trees. They — the pickles — guffawed with one another as if the world wasn't at war. While they played soldier and studied military tactics, Collier prepared for the real deal in basic training. He would graduate in early June, but this was March. Cold, wet, lonely March. She slowed for a moment, remembering his face, his embrace. The tips of her fingers rose to touch her lips in reverence of their last kiss. *Collier.*

"Whit. Wait up."

Bryant. Great. "Hey." Whitleigh spun on her heels. Bryant jogged forward, Army beret on his head.

"Can I walk you to class?"

Whitleigh pressed her lips together with a pop. "And if I say no?" She turned, walking away. He followed behind. "Figured no wouldn't stop you. Never has."

"C'mon Whit. Lighten up. We're friends." Bryant's laugh began in his stomach. "If I didn't know better, it looked like you were trying to scoot by without saying hi to me."

Caught. Whitleigh bit down on the inside of her jaw. "I haven't been too social lately. I'm trying though." She kept up a swift pace.

"I know you miss Collier. We all do." Bryant matched her steps and then some. "He had a lot of guts dropping out of college like that, especially during wartime."

Whitleigh winced and adjusted the weight of her backpack. "You gotta do what God wants you to do."

"I guess. Here, let me get that." Bryant tugged on her shoulder straps.

Whitleigh halted, turning on her heels once more, and tilted her chin upward to face Bryant. The square line of his jaw appeared more prominent as he smiled, arching his sandy blond eyebrows. "I know you're trying to be nice right now, and I appreciate it, but I also know what you're doing."

"Me?"

"Don't act innocent. What would Collier think about you hitting on me all the time?"

"You need to consider your options, that's all. Long distant relationships don't fare well, statistically speaking. And —"

"And you think you're a better choice?" She grunted. "You're so arrogant."

"Confidence is easy to mistake."

"Oh, there's no mistake on my part."

Bryant opened his mouth, but Whitleigh lifted a hand. "Listen carefully. I love Collier. You and I are friends, and yes, we went on one date, but that was a year ago, before Collier and I got back together."

"But —"

"But, as great as you are, and you of all people know how great you are, you're still the kind of guy who hits on his friend's girlfriend."

"Ouch, Whit." Bryant arched his back, pulling an invisible arrow from his heart.

Whitleigh rolled her eyes. "You'll survive."

"Did you know you're beautiful even when you're mad? And sweaty? And with no makeup on? Even with your hair all pinned up and crazy looking. You've been to kickboxing, right?"

"Bye, Bryant."

"Wait up. We're in the same class, you know."

"Yeah." Whitleigh inhaled, filling her lungs. She took her time releasing the breath. The stress remained. Maybe she should sign up for another combative elective.

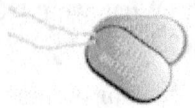

WHITLEIGH scooted into her seat with a minute to spare. Good thing too. Being late would never fly since Professor Rhine and her father went way back.

Whitleigh ignored the cheesy grin on Bryant's face. Her backpack fell to the old marble tile floor with a thud, giving her shoulders a well-deserved break. The chair next to hers — Collier's place — remained empty. Her heart sank. No matter how noble his actions, Collier dropped more than classes when he left for basic training.

She flipped open her calendar, highlighted, color coded, and scheduled to perfection. Volunteer at two. Class after. Dinner. Laundry. Work at seven. Whitleigh closed her eyes. Her breathing steadied. Strange how comforting structure felt. Safe, secure, no surprises.

"Mind if I sit?"

The sound of a voice beside her pulled Whitleigh from her daze. Reese stood, tall and willowy as ever, in a multi-patterned dress only she could pull off. Her dark eyes smiled.

Whitleigh patted Collier's seat. "I'd like some company."

"Figured. Bryant giving you a hard time again?" Reese's long fingers picked through her well-manicured afro. Bryant wiggled his fingers to wave in their direction.

Whitleigh shook her head. "I can handle him."

"And anything else that comes at you." Reese nudged at Whitleigh's side with an elbow. "One of the things I love most about you."

"It's the power of the calendar." Truth be told, planning was just as much of a pain as it was a comfort. Whitleigh crossed her legs and rested her chin in her palm.

Professor Rhine closed the thick wooden door to the classroom and stepped up to his podium, straightening his bow tie. A small ponytail gathered at the nape of his neck, held in place with a thin red ribbon. Did anyone else find it as comical as she and Collier that the man teaching European history resembled Napoleon? Whitleigh covered her smirk with an index finger.

"Let's begin." Professor Rhine pushed up his wire frame glasses and turned from the podium, walking toward the stool.

Whitleigh's stomach grumbled. Blueberry scones were tasty, but not filling. She reached in her bag for an apple, hoping to keep the crunch factor low.

"World War I, the war to end all wars, the Great War. We've talked about the logistics, the causes, the battles, the new weapons that were birthed from this global war, but today," he raised an aged finger, "I want to talk about the human element of this epic war." He wet his lips as his face came to life. "What was lost in this war?" He scanned the room of elevated hands.

Whitleigh looked away, hands on her desk. Anyone else not raising their hand? She couldn't answer with an apple in her mouth.

"You, Ms. Reese." The professor motioned with a nod of his head.

Reese lowered her hand, legs crossed. "Life was lost."

"Please explain in further detail." Professor Rhine tugged at his bow tie.

She rose, arms at her side. "Life is sacred. Taking a life should be avoided at all costs." Her voice raised a few octaves. "Soldiers were killed in horrific ways, but think about the citizens; the women who were raped and murdered. The school aged children struck by bullets or blown up because they stepped on land mines as they played in the fields. Children lost mothers and fathers." Reese folded her arms across her stomach. "There are some wars meant to be fought, but this one, Professor Rhine, should've never been."

"Thank you, Ms. Reese." The professor nodded. "You may be seated."

Reese eased back into her seat, careful to keep her short skirt in place.

"Well said." Whitleigh gave a quiet round of applause.

"Thanks."

The professor searched the room with an outstretched arm. "Anyone else want to speak up on what was taken from those affected by the Great War?"

Should she answer? Whit swallowed a chunk of apple. What would she say?

"No takers? Well then, let's play on what Reese pointed towards for a second, shall we?" Professor Rhine adjusted his glasses, pulled on his vest, and leaned forward, tipping the stool on two legs. "What justifies war and the horrific loss that ensues? Would the assassination of say, our President, or an elected official as in the case of World War I, be a worthy cause?"

"No," the class answered in unison.

"Then what?"

Whitleigh raised her hand, swallowing the bit of apple in her mouth. "If our country was invaded, then war's justifiable, like with what happened on September 11th." She twirled the stem of the apple between her fingers, her back pressed against the chair. "And I would fight for the rights of others. If someone was being persecuted in some way, it would be right to fight for them."

Professor Rhine pushed up from the stool and strolled toward the whiteboard, popping the top off of the dry erase marker. "What else? Keep 'em coming."

"Dr. Rhine, it seems like you're trying to make a point, and with all due respect, I'm not sure what you're getting at, but I don't think I like it." Bryant straightened his uniform as he rose to his feet. Reese threw a glance Whitleigh's way. She responded with a combination shrug and scowl.

"You have something you wish to say?" The professor tucked his hands behind his back.

Bryant put his hands on his hips. "My great, great grandfather lost his life in World War I. Generations of my family have served and died for our nation, and their service in life or death was valiant. They died out of obedience to their country. Our nation asked them to fight, and they did, so write that down on your whiteboard as a reason for war and all its aftermath. I'll even spell it for ya. O. B. E. D. —"

"I can spell just fine young man." Professor Rhine's glasses dropped down to the tip of his nose, but he didn't push them back into place. He glared over the frames, drilling a hole into Bryant. Whitleigh held her breath.

Bryant made his point. Professor Rhine was about to make his.

"Son, thank you for your response." He eyed the tiled floor and locked fiery eyes with Bryant. "I understand duty to our country very well. I understand obedience. I gave this nation twenty-eight years of my life." Professor Rhine nodded. "Watched my buddies blown to bits in Korea and Vietnam. A few of them captured. Those that weren't lucky enough to be killed were tortured out of their minds. Bamboo shoots shoved up their fingernails. Far more stories too terrifying and disgusting to repeat.

I bet your great, great grandfather saw similar things. If he was anything like me, then he probably did some pretty grotesque things too. Things you think you're never capable of doing until you've already done them." He licked his lips, looking away for a moment. "I live with those realities every day. You. Do. Not."

Whitleigh and Reese shared a horrified glance. Bryant stood still as stone. His Adam's apple bobbed once.

Professor Rhine cleared his throat. "I'm more than happy to serve my country when called upon, but when asked, I want to be sure of how I am to serve, and not get caught up in the patriotism as you seem to be doing, son."

Bryant looked away as the Professor continued to glare in his direction.

"Asking someone to serve should never mean unnecessary slaughter, especially at the expense of the innocent. Repercussions of war last long after the battle ends." Professor Rhine snatched a piece of scrap paper and pen from his desk and marched toward Bryant, shoving them into the young man's hands. "You, son, can write that down."

Collier's face flashed in Whitleigh's mind. What would the Army ask of Collier? Would he see horrors similar to or worse than Professor Rhine? The apple churned in her stomach, climbing up her throat. She shook and blinked a few times to shrug it off and push it down. She needed air. Her chest tightened as she hurried to gather her belongings. Whitleigh lunged from her chair, creating a clatter. With a flip of her wrist, she tossed the apple in the trash on her way out the door.

She raced down the hall and through the double glass doors until she stood beneath the dreary sky, sucking in deep breaths and exhaling sobs.

Why did he have to leave now — when the world was at war with terror? Waging a war on terror was as futile as declaring a war on evil. Why couldn't he wait until they were through with college?

Two years wasn't so far off.

"Pull yourself together." Whitleigh wiped her eyes. She

trudged over to an empty bench that had been set beneath the ancient oak tree near the center of the campus. Worse things went on in the world besides her boyfriend leaving. She worked a folded envelope from her jacket pocket, running her fingers over his name. Collier kept his promise to write while away, but would he keep his promise to come back for her? Two years, he said, and then they would marry.

Whitleigh's phone buzzed from the mesh siding of her backpack. She bent, swooping it up, flipping it open against her ear. "Hello?"

"Whit."

"Collier." Another round of tears formed in the corners of her eyes. Whitleigh didn't try to hold back her smile.

"I don't have too long."

"That's okay." Short conversations were better than none. Whitleigh folded her legs beneath her.

"Whit, I can't live another day without knowing you'll be mine forever." Collier's voice reached out and grabbed her heart.

"What are you saying?"

"Marry me, Whitleigh Haynes. After Basic."

Whitleigh's gasp caught. "I... I...." Her mind raced. So much to consider. Too much to consider. "I can't."

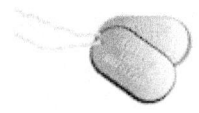

COLLIER slouched against the inside of a phone booth, one hand over his heart. The bright Fort Benning, Georgia morning sun bore down on the glass walls, allowing intensifying heat to pass through. Sweat and water dripped from the tip of his nose, splattering against the toe of his muddy boots. Slick perspiration from the morning's grueling training soaked him to the core, but Whit's response tore at his being more than the demands of any drill sergeant. Soldiers, as worn as he, stood in a long procession, quarters in hand, waiting their turn for the phone. Collier squinted, tears stinging his eyes. His dry throat cracked as he struggled for words.

"Whit." He whispered the only audible word he could manage.

"Collier... I... what about school? My scholarship? What will my mom and dad say? And what about the mission trip this summer I've been saving —"

"Please, just listen before you say anything else." Collier scratched at his head. "I've been praying about when to propose and I keep hearing now. I know it's crazy."

"Beyond."

"Tell me you don't want to marry me."

"It's not that. You know I do."

"I can take care of you, be a good husband." Collier swiped a hand over his forehead, eyebrows drawn tight. "I drew out a few pie graphs and charts. From the looks of it, I'm pretty sure I can provide a nice life for you, Whit." Collier bit his bottom lip, scratching his thumbnail over a crack in the glass.

"Pie graphs?"

"You of all people should appreciate the planning I put into this."

"Planning? You call this planning?"

Collier bobbed on the balls of his feet. "I even sent a copy of the charts to your dad. He should've gotten them by now."

"Oh, Collier."

"I wish I would've had a chance to ask your dad for your hand in marriage the proper way, but a letter is the best I can do now." The phone line remained silent. Collier wrung the metal phone cord around his wrist. "Whit, it looks like I'm going to be stationed in Colorado for a while and not Fort Campbell like we hoped."

He noted her gulp and twisted his lips to the side. She usually said more.

"Whit, you're the only one I want at my side. I don't know how often I'll be able to come see you when I'm out west for a few years, and well, long distance relationships…." he let the sentence end. "Please say something, anything."

"I want to say yes, Collier. I do… but…."

"Then say yes, Whit." Did his voice sound too pleading? "I know this isn't a proper proposal. I'm sorry about that — I am. Whit, I love you, and I know you love me. Let's take a leap of faith and do this. Be my wife Whitleigh Haynes, and make me the happiest man in the world."

"Collier."

"Whit, what's holding you back? You love me, right?"

"That's not even a question." She made a clicking noise with her mouth. "You make it sound so easy to say yes."

"It is."

Whitleigh's laugh sounded exhausted. "This isn't what we planned."

"Plans work out in a perfect world, not this one. Let go of your calendar, Whit." He rested an arm on top of the black metal phone box. "You talked about your life calling with passion—that there's something bigger out there for you. Bigger than Honduras, remember?"

Her sigh rattled the phone reception.

Collier closed his eyes and sent up a prayer.

"I'm positive there are excellent universities out in Colorado, and other scholarships. I'll make sure we have the means so you can finish and become a teacher. I want to help make that dream come true for you. Help make my dream come true and marry me."

"You're asking me to marry you in a few months, drop my summer plans, move to Colorado, and leave everything I've ever known."

"I'm asking you to take a leap of faith with me." Collier closed his eyes, sending up a prayer. *Please say yes.*

Her angst flowed through the phone alongside her fears — each one valid. Collier waited.

Whit breathed into the receiver. "I've wanted to be your wife since our first date. Even in high school, I knew." She sighed. "The way you love God and others... it motivates me. Keeps me going."

"So, you're saying?"

"I can't believe I'm doing this." She made that clicking

noise again. Collier held his breath. "Yes. Yes, I'll marry you."

"You won't regret it." Collier threw a fist in the air. "Guys, she said yes." Deep voices cheered and clapped. They took turns slapping well-wishes on Collier's back. He plugged his ears, juggling the phone between his neck and shoulder. "Baby, I have to go. My time is up."

"But, we don't have this planned out. When is the wedding? Where? How expensive is this going to be?"

"I'll call you soon." Collier grimaced under another heavy hand walloping against his back. "We'll figure it out. Maybe we could head to the courthouse."

"What? No."

"Oh, you should be getting another letter in the mail."

"But —"

"Gotta go. Love you, Babes. See in you in June at basic graduation." Collier kissed the phone and hung it up with a click. He high-fived his buddies and tried to avoid Haden's bear hug, but failed.

"You're crushing me, Haden." Collier's words wheezed. He pried his arms out of his buddy's hold. "Now it's your turn to ask Emilee."

"In good time." Haden's face lit up, too jolly for a stocky man who resembled more of a lumberjack than a soldier. "Right now we've got to turn you into wedding material."

Collier crossed his arms, one hand cupping his chin. "What's that supposed to mean?"

"You've got to be able to waltz Whit across the dance floor." Haden held a proper waltz pose and swayed.

Collier doubled over, chuckling. "Yeah, right after combatives we'll see how many guys want to take dance class with Haden the hunter."

"Laugh, but a woman wants to be romanced, pursued, and spun around a room."

"I'm romantic."

"Whatever you say," Haden grumbled, eyes crinkling around the edges. "There's always room for improvement."

"We better get moving. Formation soon." Keeping a drill sergeant waiting never turned out well. Collier broke into a jog. Haden kept up at his side. His buddy made sense about romancing Whit, sweeping her off her feet. Collier raked his teeth over his bottom lip. She deserved a proper proposal, a suitable dance partner at their wedding, and more. Much more.

RED Georgia clay covered Collier from head to toe. His arms shook with each push up. His muscles groaned in protest. Two more. One. Done. He collapsed and then rolled to his side. What a way to end the day. Whitleigh said yes and the drill sergeant said don't stop.

"C'mon Haden, you got this." Collier punched the ground in front of Haden's face.

Haden grumbled. His burly body struggled with the physical demands of basic training.

"Don't go out like this. Keep going. Remember why you're doing this."

"For me and Emilee. To pay for college. Make something of myself." Haden's words mixed with spit.

"That's right. We've all got a reason. Stay focused." Like him.

The drill sergeant marched past. "Cromwell, get away from

Deel. He's about to quit."

"No Drill Sergeant." Collier jumped to his feet, boots sinking in the mud. He stood at attention alongside his comrades. "He's just getting started."

The drill sergeant faced Collier, his nose touching the tip of Collier's nose. "Your buddy here isn't a PT stud like you. He's not cut out to be an infantryman."

"I'd rather Haden have my back in battle any day over any other soldier here, Drill Sergeant."

"That so?"

Haden mumbled and spit as he fought to complete his task. "Let it go, Collier."

Collier kept his eyes forward, careful not to eyeball the drill sergeant.

The drill sergeant prowled around Collier, eyeing him up and down. "Maybe you'd like to take your friend's spot."

Muffled gasps fell from the other cadets' mouths. Collier's heart raced within his chest. His muscles moaned. "Yes, Drill Sergeant." Collier knelt to the ground, arms shoulder length apart.

"Give me his fifty and I won't push Deel out, but," the drill sergeant cackled, "I doubt he'll make it to graduation."

Collier squared his jaw. Haden would make it, and everyone else if he had a hand in it.

Haden knelt at Collier's side. "You don't have to do this."

"You didn't have to help me shine my boots." Collier managed a sputter of words. "Or help Hiller clean toilets with a toothbrush."

"Face in the mud, Cromwell." The drill sergeant marched on, his boots fading from Collier's line-of-sight. "Get some of that Georgia clay. Tastes spot on like a peach, right?"

"Yes, Drill Sergeant." Collier licked his lips. Clay mud tasted nothing like a peach.

Haden squinted. Lines creased his forehead.

Collier clenched his teeth as his elbows bent to lower his chest to the ground. "You didn't have to help Langston peel potatoes in the chow hall either, but you did."

"Don't let him break you, Cromwell." The other soldiers rallied close. Sweat fell from the tip of Collier's nose. He lifted his eyes. Combat boots and camo pants surrounded him. They stomped the ground and cheered.

His heart swelled. These soldiers weren't his friends. They were closer. Like brothers—closer than anyone he knew from back home, except Whit, of course.

Collier pushed on and up. "I've been broken, but right now, I've never felt more whole." He sent up a prayer for strength. Strength to endure. To thrive. To be the husband to Whit that God intended, to defend his brothers, and to keep to the plan God set for him — service to Him through the military, no matter how difficult.

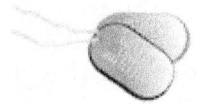

MOONLIGHT shone through the barrack windows. An owl hooted in the distance. Collier lay still, his muscles ached—more like throbbed with a heartbeat of their own. Taking Haden's load of pushups didn't appease the drill sergeant. His buddies fell asleep, warm in their bunks, way before the drill sergeant saw fit to let Collier free for the night.

More pushups. A late night run. Jogging in place while the drill sergeant threw buckets of water over his head. Insane PT torture. Who knew speaking up for a friend could hurt so bad.

So worth it. Collier cracked a smile. He didn't break. The drill sergeant tried, but by the grace of God Collier had endured.

"Thank you, Lord." His eyes closed and thoughts of Whit flooded his mind. She'd be his wife—the woman he'd share the rest of his life with. "Lord, thank you for Whit. I know she has a lot of reservations and fear, but you see her heart. She's brave and you know it as well as I do." He yawned and pulled letters and a small LED light from beneath his pillow. "Help her to see herself the way you do—fearless."

Collier thumbed through the stack of letters. Professor Rhine wrote a small history lesson on the back of a Sites of Europe postcard. Nice man. Good man.

No letters yet from his college buddies. Figures. Dudes don't really write dudes.

Whit's parents wrote. He tapped the edge of the worn envelope. Wonder if they'd respond to the letters of proposal he sent. Collier's stomach tightened and turned. He shoved the thought aside and reopened a larger envelope and slid out several sheets of paper.

The small, circular, blue light shone on the images. Crayon drawings of smiley faces, rainbows, and American flags brought a smile to Collier's face. There were many creations from Brady, even Jameson and the other kids. Mrs. Ruthers' Kindergarten class picture peeked from the pile. He held it between his fingers, taking time to scan the faces of each child whose artwork tugged at his heart. Whit sat at the end of the middle row, cuddled against the small kids who appeared all too happy to be next to her. He knew the feeling.

Mindful of his aching muscles, Collier carefully tucked the colorful pictures back into their envelope. He moved the light to the next letter, the most recent from Whit. He yawned once more and his eyes grew heavy. There could be no better way to fall asleep than with her words next to him. Her letter warmed his heart and soothed away the soreness.

Dear Collier,

I'm thinking of the last kiss we shared. Maybe I think about it too much, but it helps me to hold on to the promise that we'll be man and wife in two short years... and then we can share more than a kiss.

Collier's ears grew hot and his neck followed suit. Even after reading her words for the fifth time he couldn't push past the wave of nervous excitement. Marriage had many benefits, and now, those perks were mere months away, not years. He wet his lips and continued to read.

I'm glad we've kept ourselves pure.

It wasn't without difficulty. Collier swallowed, but his cotton dry mouth made it trying.

To say and know we'll be each other's one and only... well, that's something special-a gift from God.

Yes, it was. Collier nodded.

While he and Whit set boundaries regarding their physical relationship and gave their friends full authority to keep them accountable, there seemed to be none amongst the soldiers. Pornographic images floated around the barracks and behind the drill sergeants' backs with a consistency that both tempted and repulsed him. Looking away proved a challenge, but he and Haden kept each other accountable. Collier blew out a short breath and read on.

Things are good here, even though I miss you a ton and a half. I do have more grumpy days than usual-Bryant helps bring those on, but Reese and Lennon snap me out of it.

Bryant. Collier narrowed his eyes. Friend or not, Bryant

better keep his distance from Whit.

Classes are going. Twenty-one hours this semester may not have been the best idea with my schedule, but that's why I have an awesome calendar.

The kids at the elementary school are beyond ready for Spring Break. I'll miss seeing their sweet faces for a whole week. I won't know what to do with myself. Poor Mrs. Ruthers looks like she needs the break more than any of the kids! I wonder if I'll look like that after becoming a teacher. Ha!

Brady's dad is coming home on leave soon. You should see how happy he is. The whole class has been making cards, letters, and care packages for him and his unit. I know you keep telling me you're safe, but between Brady's dad, and Professor Rhine's war stories and lectures, I find myself praying more for your safety and for what the future may hold you... for us....

Collier rubbed at his shoulder. The muscle tightened at his touch. Training to be a soldier left little time to worry about anything else, especially war, but Whit's prayers were always welcome and appreciated.

We've been swamped at The Feeding Trauf. By the way, Andy says the owner is considering correctly spelling the name.

Finally. Collier held in a chuckle. His ribs throbbed and he winced.

Seems like they've won some best BBQ contest and he wants to give off a more professional appearance.

Thought you'd appreciate that, and I thought you'd like to know that I've raised enough money to go to Honduras! Sold several more picture frames and racked up extra tips to help make it happen. Am I nervous? Terribly! Unsure? Still a little, but, Honduras it is!

Something to think about... I almost have enough money to cover the cost of someone else's trip... maybe you could come with me? Still have your passport, right? Not sure how many days you get off after you graduate basic.

Collier arched a brow. He did still have his passport from last year's mission trip to Jamaica. Perhaps he could go-after the wedding, or before? Collier twisted his mouth to the side. He could think on that when he had more brain power.

It's getting late, so I'll close with this:

I love you more than:

1: Chocolate

2: My favorite pair of warm fuzzy socks (Yes, the ones with holes)

3: Climbing trees

4: The Kentucky Wildcats basketball team (Go Big Blue)

5: All the books on my bookshelf, minus the Bible of course

6: All my crafting supplies, yes, even glitter!!

7: Picnics

8: Classic Rock music, oh yes, even Credence Clearwater Revival (That's a lot of love going on there)

9: Antique stores! Believe it, it's true!

10: Myself. I will always love you more than myself.

Always!
Love me always,
Whit, your Sweat Pea

Collier kissed the pink lip prints on top of the page. He smiled and closed his eyes with the letter tucked next to his side. Sleep welcomed him. His aching muscles relaxed. Images of Whit accompanied rest like a close friend. Her smile, her laugh. The way she danced as she walked. She hummed a tune as she rode shotgun in his Ford pickup. That long blond hair swirled in the wind. No, there wasn't a better way to fall asleep.

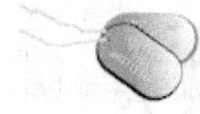

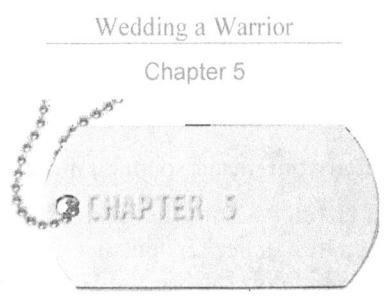

CHAPTER 5

LETTERS stamped, stacked, folded, opened, and worn, piled around Whitleigh. She sat on the cold dorm room floor, legs crossed and glue stick in hand, ready to scrapbook. If only she could concentrate. Her brain hurt. Thoughts swirled and swerved at super speeds through the freeway system of her mind.

Whitleigh wet her lips. Collier proposed this morning. She said yes. No, it wasn't a dream.

Her fingers worked through the pages of the Kindergarten scrapbook with a mind of their own. Twinkling lights dangled from black and white tulle curtains hanging above the only window in the room. Her waitress apron hung on a hook near her half closet, washed and ironed, ready for her next shift. The painted cinder block walls displayed both posters and photographs in frames of various shapes and colors.

Reese tapped a pen against the side of her mouth and lounged in a pink beanbag chair. She flipped through budget building papers. Lennon typed away at her pint-sized corner desk. Her eyes fixed on the computer screen, tongue peeping through her lips. Each week, Lennon devised multiple plans for creating fresh water wells around the world. A corner of Whitleigh's mouth lifted. College life and ideals for a better world consumed her friends, not weddings, or marriage, or war.

Whitleigh blew out a burst of air, raking a hand through her hair.

Yes.

That three letter word meant so much more.

She lifted an envelope from the tallest stack. Collier nailed the timing of his latest letter. It met her in the mailbox after morning classes. Whitleigh sat back, elbow propped up on her refurbished thrift store footstool. She opened the letter, holding it with both hands, soaking in the scent of the parchment, fresh and earthy, like Collier. Rereading it soothed wedding jitters.

Dear Whit,

The paracord ring is temporary. I'm counting on a yes, and will make sure you have a nice, big engagement ring to show off to your friends. God's got huge plans for our lives. I'm writing under the light of a headlamp, so forgive my writing and the shortness of this letter. I want you to know that I love you even more than...

1: Fried chicken

2: Beef tips over rice

3: Ice cream sandwiches (the Neapolitan kind)

4: Sweet tarts

5: Video games

6: Football

7: Myself. I will always love you more than myself.

Love always,

Collier, Your Soldier Boy

WHITLEIGH chuckled and twirled the olive colored paracord ring around her left ring finger. This particular "I love you more than…" list consisted of many more food items than usual. The poor man must be starving. With care, Whitleigh folded the note, tucked it in the envelope, and added it to the photo box underneath her bunk. She sighed, running a hand over the box — a portion of their love story. Another segment of their lives was soon to come. Her face warmed and she pushed up the sleeves of her worn Kentucky Wildcat hoodie.

A wad of paper smacked against the side of her face. "Earth to Whitleigh." Reese pursed her lips. "Are you tutoring tomorrow? I was hoping to hitch a ride with you in the morning." She shook a folder with way too much enthusiasm. "Want to get these flyers out to all the elementary teachers to give to the students' parents."

Whitleigh reached out for the folder, scanning the flyers. "Free personal finance classes. I think it's great you're doing that."

"Doing my best to make a difference in the community. The library is letting me host a free course once a week." Reese wiggled her fingers in the air. "So how about that ride?"

"You know you don't have to ask. We leave at 8."

"So early." Reese grumbled, but nodded. "Oh, and my mom wants to order a few painted picture frames. She really liked what you did with the ones on your wall. Would you have time to get them done by next weekend?"

Next weekend. Whitleigh chewed on her thumbnail, eyeing the calendar by her bedside. Bold red lines slashed through the days, counting down until Collier returned. "Um, I think I can do that."

Lennon spun in her seat. "When?" Her spiraling red hair bounced with each shake of her head. "In between classes, waitressing, tutoring, and painting a whole slew of other things for people? You've raised enough money. Why are you working so hard?"

"Good question." Whitleigh slouched and smooshed her cheek in the palm of her hand.

"Lennon's right, Whit." Reese pouted and crossed her lanky legs at the ankle, sinking deeper into the beanbag chair. "Mom's order can wait. You've got to rest too, you know."

Rest. Yeah, right. Whitleigh gathered her knees to her chest.

"You still feeling bad?" Reese looked from Whitleigh to Lennon. "She ran out of class this morning. Ate a bad apple."

"I'm fine."

Lennon slid from her chair and onto the floor next to Whitleigh. "Spill it. What's bugging you? I knew something was wrong when your cardigan collection was out of color sequence."

"I really need to work on this. I want each kid to have their very own book." Whitleigh tapped the pile of colorful paper on the floor. Her fingers surfed along the binding of the scrapbook.

"I know that look on your face. You're either gonna cry or laugh." Reese pried her body from the leathery beanbag chair and huddled on Whitleigh's side. "Hey, Collier's okay. He'll be back, you'll see. And if you're still worried about going to Honduras —"

"I so want to go," Lennon shrieked, fingers curled in the air. "Dumb wisdom teeth depleted me."

"Anyway, as I was saying," Reese shot a glare in Lennon's direction, "if you're still scared to go…" her voice trailed.

Whitleigh scrunched her nose. They'd find out soon enough

anyway. "This morning Collier called and asked me to marry him. I said yes." The words poured forth, sounding more insane when spoken out loud.

"What?" Reese screeched like a barnyard owl. "When? How?" She snatched Whitleigh's left hand, gawking at the sturdy cord around her ring finger.

"I'll have a real one soon." Whitleigh's stomach knotted. She rolled the ring around her finger. "But honestly, I like this one just as much as a diamond."

"When are you getting married?" Reese clasped Whitleigh's hands between hers, eyes bulging.

"This summer." Whitleigh groaned, but couldn't fight the urge to giggle. "Three months, maybe less."

"You're just now telling us?" Lennon's mouth formed a perfect oval. "What did your parents say? This is crazy, you know that, right?"

"I'm sorry. Ugh." Whitleigh swatted at a piece of loose hair dangling in her face. "I've been trying to process it all day, and no," Whitleigh clenched her teeth, shoulders hovering beneath her ears, "I haven't told Mom and Dad yet, but I'm pretty sure they'll be calling soon."

Reese tugged at Whitleigh's elbow. "Have you prayed about this?"

Whitleigh nodded and nudged her planner with her foot. That thing was a blessing and a curse. "The timing isn't what I wanted, or anything like we planned, but... God's got this, and it's going to be fine." That's right. Whitleigh dipped her head up and down. Her shoulders relaxed, the tension from the day melted away. She allowed herself another giggle. Mrs. Whitleigh Cromwell fit well.

"This is so romantic. Crazy, but romantic." Lennon clasped her hands together and released a whimsical sigh. "A man in uniform proposing, sweeping you off your feet. A phone call that changed the direction and destiny of your lives."

Whitleigh's face contorted. Reese sat as still as her stony expression.

"What?" Lennon folded her arms. "I'm interested in relationship stuff too." She flipped the cascade of red curls away from her shoulder. "I just haven't found the right guy yet."

Right. Ms. Brainiac interested in dating? Whitleigh poked at Lennon's knee. "I can hook you up with Bryant."

"Or Blaine." Reese lifted a hand.

"Um, yeah, no. That whole twin thing freaks me out. I can see Bryant pretending to be Blaine when we're out and ugh, that's gross." Lennon shuddered for good reason.

"Look for the scar." Whitleigh pointed to the corner of her forehead. "Blaine has a small one right there. Bryant hit him in the head with a screwdriver when we were little. Bled forever. Poor guy."

Lennon grimaced. "It's always the nice ones that take the beating."

"True story." Whitleigh shoved the twins from her mind, especially Bryant and his flirty ways, and continued to toy with her impromptu engagement ring.

"So, Whit, what are you gonna do?" Reese scooted closer. The scent of her mint chewing gum filled the space between them.

Lennon folded her legs, chin resting on closed fists.

"I guess I'm going to plan a wedding." Whitleigh sank her face into her palms, breathing in and out. She lifted her head. "In three months. Without a set date."

"Talk about a mission impossible." Lennon snorted, smacking at the floor. "It took my sister a year to plan her wedding and she was insane the whole time."

"We can do this." Reese scrambled to her feet, snatched up Whitleigh's calendar, and reached for a pen and notepad. "We'll make a checklist. Don't consider us just your roommates anymore—we're your personal wedding planners." She scribbled, taking time to tap her bottom lip with the pen. "Bridesmaids: Reese and Lennon, check. Venue. Dress. Cake. Caterers. Photographer. Flowers."

"How do I even pay for a wedding? Mom and Dad won't be able to cover the cost of everything." There weren't many people left in Collier's family to ask for help. "I can't use the money for Honduras, and anything left pays for my gas and car insurance."

Whitleigh followed Reese and Lennon's line of sight. Their eyes fixed on the large water cooler bottle filled with loose change and tip money at the foot of her bed. "No way, guys." She fanned her hands. "I've been saving that since I was fifteen."

"Times like these call for a sacrifice, Whit." Lennon placed a firm hand on Whitleigh's shoulder.

"That's the money I'm using to furnish my classroom. Cute chairs, cushions, an entire library section with audio books available. The latest technology for my students." Whitleigh's voice squeaked more than she intended. "This money could change the lives of my students. Their future is counting on this."

"Hello there Ms. Dramatic." Reese mimicked Whitleigh's words with puppeteer-like hand movements. "You've got two years until you get a classroom of your own, maybe longer in this economy." She crossed her legs, hand pointed at Whitleigh. "It boils down to the fact that you're worried about how to pay for a wedding when you have probably a few grand sitting there."

"It's a no brainer." Lennon nodded in agreement with Reese.

Whitleigh clamped her cheeks between her palms. "I hate

when you guys are right."

Lennon hopped up, dusting off her jeans and Lord of the Rings T-shirt. She skipped over the scrapbook pile and landed next to the water cooler bottle. No matter how deep her grunts or the intensity with which she tugged, the container did not budge. "A little help ladies."

Whitleigh stood and dawdled forward. She and Reese pushed and pulled alongside Lennon, all three spewing variations of disgruntled groans. The oversized plastic bottle sat like a strong-willed child.

If only Collier was here to help. Whitleigh kicked at the container. "How are we going to get this money to the bank if we can't even lift it?"

"I hate to say it ladies." Reese gritted her teeth as she pushed the bottle with her feet. "This is a job for Bryant and his friends."

"No way." Lennon made a final grunt. The container toppled over, spilling out a steady stream of coins. "We take a little at a time. Grab some zip top bags, Whit."

Whitleigh scanned the petite pantry shelf under her elevated bed and snatched several plastic bags. The green screen of her cell phone lit up with an angry buzz.

Two lumps rose in her throat. Mom and Dad. "Hey girls, I'm gonna have to take this call. Can you two step out for a few?"

Lennon and Reese nodded. "Good luck," they whispered before shuffling out the door.

She'd need it.

The door snapped closed. Whitleigh cradled the buzzing phone for a moment before answering.

"Hey Momma." She licked her lips, eyes closed. No need to be nervous. "You're here? On campus?" Whitleigh's eyes shot open. She pulled her hair to the side, knotting it around her fingers. "You're here right now? Dad's with you too?" She choked on a gulp. "Yes, I know we need to talk. Be right down." She slid into a pair of worn glittered flats and stepped from the room, head held high. A difficult conversation awaited.

"**WE** can go somewhere else to talk. Anywhere." The coffee house. Library. Somewhere public. A place with witnesses. Whitleigh ran a hand up and down her arm. Sweat bubbled up on the back of her neck. They loved Collier, but how would they feel about her marrying him in a matter of months?

"Your room is fine, dear." Momma stepped into the dorm. She hugged Whitleigh close and sniffled. Her soft brown curls tickled the tip of Whitleigh's nose. "Tell Reese and Lennon the next time we come down, we'll take all of you out to eat."

"Who can say no to a free meal?" Did her laugh sound too nervous? Whitleigh pressed her lips together.

Dad stood behind Momma, a head taller, silent, and hands planted in his pants' pockets. When had his dark hair become speckled with gray? Whitleigh bowed her head as Momma released the embrace. Dad reached for her left hand, holding it carefully in his. His hands, rough and weather worn, scratched beneath her palm. Dad's eyes glistened as he examined the paracord engagement ring. Whitleigh raked her teeth over her bottom lip. Her heart raced.

"So, you said yes, then?" His brow line crinkled.

Whitleigh managed a nod. Sometimes no words said more.

His skin, though red by nature — a true mark of a construction worker — paled in seconds. Momma lifted a tissue from her shirt pocket and held it to her nose. Short lines stretched from the corners of her brown eyes, touching the tops of her cheeks. Her makeup didn't hide red puffy eyes well.

Dad coughed, looking from the coins spilled across the floor and back to Whitleigh. Her hand still lay in his. "Whit, I know since you've become a young woman, I haven't really been, well, the father you needed me to be. I've been busy, working, and gone a lot."

"It's okay, Daddy." Whit looked away. He was right. Since she started the transition from a young lady to a woman, her father, the man of few words, became a man of even fewer words — and less hugs.

"I'm sorry, Whit. I should've been there more for you. I got my priorities messed up for a while, but I know now work is a poor substitute for family." Dad's Adam's apple bobbed. He swallowed and wiped at his eyes. "Be honest. Are you marrying Collier to fill a void that I may have created in your life?"

"What?" Whitleigh flinched. She pulled her hand from his. "You've been a great dad — still are. Just hug me more and take me fishing like you used to." She smiled, lightening the tense moment.

Dad nodded, wrapping his arms around Whitleigh. "You've grown up too fast."

Momma circled a hand over Whitleigh's back. She sighed as the stress melted from her shoulders. Back rubs were one of the many things she missed from home.

"Are you sure about this, sweetheart?" Momma sat on the bed, patting the mattress at her side.

Whitleigh sat. "I'm scared, but certain."

"Army life is no joke." Dad scratched at his brows with a thumb. He took a seat on the other side of Whitleigh. The bed sank under their weight. "There's a war going on. Collier is an infantry soldier, Whit. He's training to fight. Battle can do things to a man. My father, well, you've heard the stories of what war did to him and what he did to us in return."

Yes. Horrible abuse. Whitleigh nodded, head hung. Professor Rhine's morning monologue regarding the hells of war scrolled through her thoughts in broken snippets. She cringed, closing her eyes for a moment.

"We love Collier, Whit." Momma brushed Whitleigh's hair from her face. Whitleigh's skin tingled as Momma's fingernails skimmed over her shoulder. "We've known him since he was born. Been like a son to us."

True. Collier and his brother spent many nights with them when Mr. Cromwell came home from the bars looking for a fight. Whitleigh rested her chin on top of a closed fist.

"But, Whit, honey, you're so young." Young. Yes, she supposed so, but what did age matter anyway? Momma looked into Whitleigh's eyes. Her brown eyes pleaded and looked similar to Whitleigh's in shape only.

Dad patted Whitleigh's knee. "No matter what age you get married, or how ready you think you are, marriage takes a lot of work under any circumstances." He pushed the tips of his fingers together. "You're not just marrying Collier."

Whitleigh lifted her head, eyes squinted. "What do you mean?"

"You're marrying the military too." His face grew solemn. "And that can add a lot of other challenges to a marriage."

Moving cross country and all that it entailed seemed challenging enough. Did even more obstacles lay waiting? Whitleigh's stomach churned. Obstacles like the horrors of war?

Momma lifted Whitleigh's chin with an index finger, her smile warming. "Plans change on a whim in the military. A lot of hurry up and wait. For a planner like you, that could be difficult to handle."

"I'm not pretending to know what to expect, but that's faith, right? Stepping out on nothing to stand on something." Whitleigh sat tall, shoulders back. "I'm trying to do what God wants, and believe me, it's hard." She lowered her head for a moment. "In my faith I've been so careful, so calculated. I've felt more like a cowardly lion than one that roars." Her chest rose with her voice. "I want to roar. I want to live... really live, and do those things that scare me to death."

Her parents stood motionless, their expressions firm. Whitleigh held her breath, her palms dampened.

Momma leaned in and placed a kiss on Whitleigh's cheek. "Then roar, baby girl."

Whitleigh exhaled. She smiled so big her cheeks hurt.

"That's my girl." Dad rubbed the top of Whitleigh's head. She slouched under the weight of his hand. At least he forwent the noogies.

Dad leaned forward, reaching into his back pocket. With one smooth motion, he pulled out two tattered envelopes. Whitleigh's cheeks grew warm. Collier's letters. She swallowed hard.

"Collier's got a pretty nice game plan."

Momma chuckled. "His graphs are impressive."

"We couldn't pick a finer man than Collier for you." Dad rubbed a hand over his mouth. "I would've liked it better if he had asked me in person, but I guess under the circumstances, and if you're sure, then it's settled."

"I'm certain." Certain but terrified.

"So. He's sure you'll be stationed in Colorado?" Momma dabbed at her eyes. "I've heard it's lovely out there." His voice squeaked. "Collier promises he will see to it you finish college. I know he'll take care of you."

"He will. That's Collier. It's what he does." Whitleigh

smirked. "And I'm sure you'll love visiting us out there."

"Professor Rhine was stationed out at Fort Carson for a long time." Dad squinted as if in thought.

"So I've heard. I know way too much about his life experiences." Whitleigh chuckled past a gulp.

"Sweet girl, you know we'd offer you the moon if we could afford it, but —"

"Don't worry, Daddy. I think I can cover the cost of the wedding, and I'm sure Collier will send money, too."

Momma bent over, scooping up a handful of coins. "But, Whit."

"I know." Whitleigh sighed, her smile slight. Her shoulders lifted and fell. "It's gonna be worth it."

"We have a little to offer." Dad cupped his chin. "Your mom and I know how much you like our old barn. We thought maybe if we could get it ready in time, we could have the wedding there."

Whitleigh couldn't contain the laugh leaping from her mouth. She grabbed her parents' hands.

Momma gave a tight squeeze. "Maybe we can have the reception in the field."

"A rustic wedding!" Whitleigh gasped, her mouth opening. "Perfect."

"I can make about anything you need, too." Dad dropped an elbow to his knee. "Lots of scrap wood lying around. I can cut a tree or two down if need be."

Her heart leapt in several directions. Whitleigh lunged, swallowing her parents with her arms.

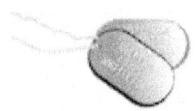

CHAPTER 6

MAY 9th

Dear Collier,

There's so much I want to tell you. I'm busting at the seams with excitement. I can't wait to see you again. Every day I look more and more forward to becoming your wife. We're doing it Babes—stepping out on faith, taking this journey together. Ha! It's an incredible feeling... like going upside down on a roller coaster but way more awesome. I'll fill you in on the wedding details when you call, but all is going according to plan, which I admit helps me sleep better at night.

So, the Honduras trip has been pushed back to the end of July. Guess there was some scheduling issues? I know you told me you only had thirty days of leave after basic training graduation until you had to report to duty in Colorado. That means you probably won't be able to go. I'm prepared not to go if you'd rather me stay in Colorado with you, but I'd like to go—crazy, I'm saying that, right? The more I pray about it, the more peace I feel about going—no more fear, or worry! We can talk more about it.

I made it through this semester. Whew! I know school's over, but I couldn't give up going to the elementary school. They've got a few weeks left. I don't mind staying to help and I really want to celebrate the end of the year with them. We're going to make confetti-filled balloons and have a water balloon war! I haven't told the kids that I won't be back next year... that's gonna break my heart, but Colorado is beautiful, and we'll have a happy life there together. So many places to see out west! Let the adventures begin!

Gotta get to work, oh, and it's officially The Feeding Trough... so much more classy. Andy said he's gonna send you a picture of the new name. Ha! That's one to keep.

I love you more than:

Bubble gum, The Feeding Trough's new name (Ha!), root beer in a glass bottle, old-time movies, popcorn, rainy day afternoon naps, and myself—I'll always love you more than myself.

Love me always,
Whit

THE middle of May. Week ten of fourteen in basic training and AIT—Advanced Individual Training. Almost done. Collier slashed through another day on the pocket-sized calendar. He flipped over to June, eyes tracing the green circle around Saturday the 28th — their wedding day, just two weeks after basic graduation. Collier tucked the calendar in his Bible and bent over, placing it in his rucksack under the bottom bunk. His dog tags pressed against his tan T-shirt like a light weight. Sweat rings created half circles under his arms. Georgia might as well be on the equator. The open barrack window and warm breeze provided little relief from the heat of the day.

Collier sat on the edge of his bed, Whit's letter in hand. He couldn't help but smirk. She was doing it, becoming brave and fearless. God answered his prayer. Collier laughed to himself. The scent of Sweet Pea floated from the paper and whirled around his head. He breathed it in. Soon he'd hold her in his arms again.

Collier flipped through several pictures tucked in the envelope at his side — silly faces, their friends hanging out, splashing in the fountain on campus. A bunch of crazies. Collier smiled. Did Bryant have to have an arm around Whit? Collier frowned and rolled his eyes. His thumb rounded over Whit's cheerful expression. Blond hair, blue eyes. His Whit. He slipped a notebook and pen from his pillowcase and penned a letter to her. Before sending it off, he'd add cash. Even though Whit was managing well enough on her own so far, weddings were expensive.

Haden hopped from his top bunk and rummaged through his pillowcase. "Gum?" He pulled out a stick of Big Red, offering it to Collier.

"No thanks. It's hot enough in here without setting my mouth on fire." Collier grinned, shaking his head at Haden. He kept the craziest things in his pillow.

Collier tucked his photos and letters away.

Soldiers scrambled around the room, tidying up the area. Drill sergeants often entered unannounced, ready to yell at the slightest speck of dust. Order, discipline, respect, and obedience — that's what they demanded. That's what Collier delivered.

"Orders go out today." Haden crammed two pieces of gum in his mouth. "We find out for sure where our first duty station will be."

"I'm not sure how much it will change." Collier smoothed out the wrinkles on his bed and tightened the sheets on each corner. "They acted like it was set in stone last time."

"I guess." Haden shoved the gum back in his pillowcase and gave his bed a once over. He folded his arms, leaning up against the metal bed railing. "How do you get your sheets so tight like that? Not a wrinkle."

"Paracord." He pushed his hands in his pockets and shrugged.

"No way."

"Shh." Collier lifted a finger to his mouth. "Don't let the drill sergeant catch on. Here. Look." Collier lifted the edge of his thin mattress with ease. "I've tied a cord to the bottom of the sheet at each corner, pulled it tight, and then tied it like you would your shoes." "Wow." Haden examined the route of the parallel threads. "Genius."

"I've got a few good ideas like that." Collier laid the mattress back in place. It bounced a time or two. The springs creaked and rattled.

"Since you've got a knack for paracord uses, you should think about making a bunch of those bracelets as party favors."

"Party favors?"

"For your wedding."

"Oh." Okay. Collier wiped a bead of sweat from his forehead. "I thought people who come to our wedding bring me and Whit gifts, not the other way around."

Haden huffed, shaking his head. He rolled his eyes.

"What?" Collier landed a teasing punch on Haden's shoulder. "Why do you know so much about wedding stuff anyway?"

The burliest men were filled with surprises.

"Emilee's family owns a wedding planning business." Haden rubbed at his arm, grimacing. "Anyway, the paracord bracelets would be a nice touch. Tied with a small ribbon with the Scripture verse about how a strand of three cords cannot be easily broken."

"But I make them with two cords."

"You know what I mean." He knelt, swiping a few specks of dust from his boots. "Just make the bracelets."

"Sounds like a job my best man might want to help me with."

"Fine, but I'm stealing your paracord bed making idea."

The heavy barrack door flew open. "Attention."

The men scrambled into position at the end of their bunks, eyes straight ahead, fixed on anything but the drill sergeant.

"This won't take long." The drill sergeant flipped papers on his clipboard. "Going in alphabetical order, I'm calling last name and the placement of your first duty assignment." He cleared his throat and marched through the ranks. "Aaron, Korea. Anderson, Korea. Blevins, Hawaii."

Collier kept the heels of his boots together. Whit would love Colorado and sounded excited about the location. Nature at its best. Historical sites to visit. He allowed himself a short sigh.

"Cromwell, Korea. Deel, Korea."

What? Collier's jaw muscles tensed. Did he hear that right? He dared not break rank to protest. Korea? What happened to Colorado?

Collier took the risk and eyed Haden. His widened eyes gave proof of pure shock.

Korea. They both were headed to Korea. Collier tried to

swallow.

The drill sergeant marched on like the smashed pieces of Collier's plans weren't in his way.

Heat pulsed through Collier's veins. Breathe. His heart sank to the pit of his stomach. *Whit.* Would she still want to marry him after she knew?

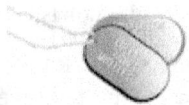

COLLIER wiped both hands over his face. He stood in the phone booth, staring at the phone as if it would dial itself. Three days since he'd received word of the drastic change of plans. Korea. Whit needed to hear. He needed to call, so why could he only stand there?

"You can do this, Collier." Haden's large hand palmed Collier's shoulder. "Emilee took it better than I thought. So will Whit. Call."

"But what if —"

"Call."

Collier lifted the phone from the receiver. Smudged fingerprints and dirt covered the phone. He scrubbed it clean with the cuff of his Army fatigues. The small metal numbers clicked as he dialed.

Haden patted his back and stepped away. "I'll be over here if you need me."

Collier managed a nod. His throat tightened with each ring.

"Hello?" Whit sounded upbeat. "Collier?"

"H… Hey." His words fought through the desert conditions of his mouth. "It's good to hear your voice."

"Back at ya." She giggled. "Got a lot of exciting things to

tell you."

"Oh yeah." He licked his lips. He needed good news right about now. "Care to share?"

"Did you get my letter? Well, for starters, wedding plans are better than I ever imagined." She talked so fast. "Reese and Lennon are pros, and Mom and Dad are amazing. I can't wait for you to see the barn. It's gorgeous. Professor Rhine's been over here helping Dad almost every day since school let out." Whitleigh smacked her lips together. "It's never been weird having him around until he became my teacher."

Collier sank his teeth into his bottom lip. Her daddy was gonna kill him for breaking her heart, and Professor Rhine would probably flunk him if he could. Collier nodded and regained focus. "How are we doing on cash?"

"$3,326.56 remaining after the dress, flowers, and cake deposit. The flowers are lovely. Simple, but beautiful. Lavender, in mason jars, maybe some lilac worked in with lace, burlap, and a few pearls." Whitleigh's voice grew louder as the words sped from her mouth. Collier listened, enjoyed her enthusiasm even if he couldn't get too excited over lace and purple flowers, or the news he needed to tell. "Right now we're working out prices with the catering school. Since Lennon and Reese are doing the desserts we only need a few appetizers from the caterers. Nothing fancy. I'm thinking a potato bar with yummy toppings."

Potato bar? Collier allowed himself a contained snicker. Might as well enjoy a good moment before a bad. "I still can't believe you had almost five grand in change."

"Crazy, right?"

"I can send more money if you need me to."

"Right now we're good. Save your money so we'll have a nice cushion to start married life with."

"So, um, what's left to buy?" Delaying the purpose of the

call couldn't last much longer.

"The honeymoon." She twirled her voice, low and flirty.

Their honeymoon. Collier gulped, his brows lifted. "Oh." That part of their relationship, the part he worked hard not to think about — the intimate portion. Waiting was right. Right, but difficult. He swallowed and cleared his throat.

"Reese's mom is a travel agent. She's got a great deal at a resort in Niagara Falls. It's just for a few days, but for the price, we can't beat it."

"Book it."

"Done." She giggled and his cheeks flushed. "A few days is really all we'll need anyway. Especially since we'll be in Colorado. That's a honeymoon in and of itself."

Collier coughed, clearing his mind more than his throat. "I'm good with Niagara Falls." Or anywhere. He coughed once more.

"And guess what else?" Her excitement poured through the phone. "I've been accepted into the University of Colorado at Colorado Springs with a partial scholarship." She squealed. Collier pulled the phone from his ear. His stomach turned. All her planning, for what? "I've been waiting to tell you. Figured I can work to help make up the difference and hold off on taking out any loans. They've got a great teaching program too." Her sigh carried too much enthusiasm for the news on the tip of his tongue. "Everything is falling into place."

"I know you were nervous about saying yes to me." He brushed a hand over the back of his neck. "It makes me happy to hear your excitement now." If only for a few more seconds.

"I spent too much time worrying about all the what-if's. This whole taking a leap of faith thing is great."

Collier held his breath. He toyed with the metal phone cord and chewed on the inside of his jaw. "Whit, baby, I, um…."

"Have to go again? I understand."

"I, uh, have to tell you something."

"All ears."

"I'm being stationed in Korea." He paused, closing his eyes. "Not Colorado."

Whit released a quick gasp. Collier hung his head, heart racing. His chest throbbed. Whit remained silent.

"It's for a year. Unaccompanied." He shifted his weight. His fingers pressed against the glass wall of the booth. "We can still get married in June. You can visit me anytime, and I get to take leave too, so I can visit you."

"But I can't live there with you?"

"Not this time."

"What about school?" Her voice shook. "Collier, I gave up my scholarship to transfer to Colorado. What now?"

He ran a hand over his crew cut and released a long sigh. No solutions came to mind.

She sniffled.

"Don't cry, Whit."

"What am I supposed to do, Collier?"

The phone grew heavy in his hand. The fun conversation had been replaced by the sound of tears.

"Whit?"

"Let's forget this Collier. The wedding's off."

"Whit. No. Please. Wait." Her harsh words bit and sent a chill over his body. He stumbled back and leaned against the phone booth door.

"I can't believe this is happening."

"Me neither Whit, but let's figure this out together." He tapped his fingers on the window. "Don't leave. We're meant to be together and you know it."

"Collier, don't."

"So what if there's a kink in our plan? When have our plans ever worked anyway?" He chuckled, pressing a palm against his forehead.

"I can't do this right now. It's too much."

"Don't hang up. Please." Collier raised his hand. "It's a lot to take in. I know."

She whimpered and his heart writhed inside his chest.

"I'm asking a lot of you. I want you to be my wife, I do. I understand me going away for a year could change things."

"Could? Collier it does."

He pressed his lips together. *Don't give her permission to go.* "Whit. I love you, and I, uh…" *Don't let her go.* "How about we take a few days to think things through. If we can't come to a solution regarding school, and me being away for a year, or if you feel you… you… can't go through with the wedding right now, it's okay." He washed his hand over his brows. "I'll wait for you forever. You'll have to be the one to end us, because I won't. I can't."

Her quiet sobs played a painful tune in his ear.

"I never wanted to hurt you, Whit. I've always wanted to do the right thing, follow God."

"Is this what He wants? For us to be apart?"

Collier shook his head. Sometimes there were no easy answers. "I'll give you time to think things through, Whit, and," he bit at his fist, "I'll understand whether or not you decide to marry me, wait, or," his stomach lurched, "or if you decide it's over."

The whistle blew. Time for weapons class. "Whit?"

"I know. You gotta go."

The story of their lives.

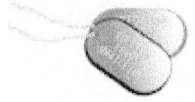

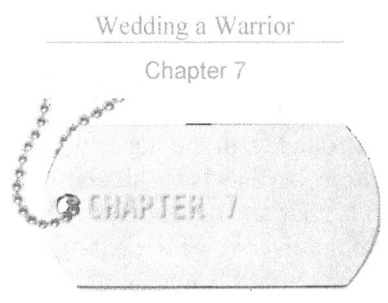

WHITLEIGH slid the phone into the back pocket of her blue jean shorts. She pressed her back against her parents' aged and grayed barn. The last bit of air escaped her lungs. Rigid slivers of the damaged wood grated against her shoulder blades. Could she still marry Collier? Her head spun.

Collier's bombshell gave her much to consider. Were they over? The paracord ring clung to her finger. A future without him by her side flashed in broken, uneven spurts through her imagination. She sucked in a sharp breath, cradling her arms around her waist. Tears dotted her eyes. Whitleigh wiped them away with the back of her hand and tossed her long braid over her shoulder.

Dad hammered away, working hard to whip the old barn into wedding condition. A few playful robins flew past the twisted honeysuckle vines climbing the side of the barn. Whitleigh eyed the afternoon sky. Puffs of cotton clouds hung against the blue background. The day was too pretty for bad news.

Her chin dimpled. She sniffed, wiping at her nose. Crying never helped. She scanned the land around her, biting at her lip, praying for a distraction or maybe an escape from reality.

Professor Rhine's beat up Ford pickup sat parked in the gravel drive. At his age, he wasn't much help with manual labor, but he kept Dad company. They chatted back and forth about rental properties and renovations, a topic to which they both related. Momma strolled from the house toward the barn, a tray of fresh lemonade in her hands. Whitleigh took cover, putting the barn between herself and her mother. Once behind the barn, she headed toward the river at the bottom of the hill. Best no one knew now, at least not until she got a grip on her emotions.

"Where's Whit?" Her momma called out.

The men mumbled.

"Well, if you see her, let her know her friends are on their way. Good news for you. Looks like you need a few more hands."

Whitleigh hurried down the hillside. Tall green grass smacked across her shins. She kicked her leather cowboy boots from her feet and buried her toes into the muddy riverbank. Fresh earthy scents whirled about in the slight breeze. Slow, clear, and steady water flowed down the shallow river. Nothing hindered the current, except maybe a piece of driftwood tangled up in overgrown weeds and vines. The water didn't mind. It flowed anyway, pushing past the obstacle with ease. Could she make herself as carefree as a river, overcoming whatever challenge lay in her path?

She sat, arms dangling over her knees. A few more tears trickled down her cheeks. "What do I do, Lord?"

No answer.

"Do I let him go? What about school?"

No reply.

Whitleigh fanned the grass dancing at her calves. The blades ran between her fingers. Leaves rustled overhead in the late spring wind. Branches from a nearby weeping willow swayed to the beat of a silent melody. Sunlight danced on top of the water.

"I'm waiting." Whitleigh tilted her head, ear pointed toward heaven.

"Hey."

Whitleigh jumped, looking over her shoulder. Bryant ambled down the hill in her direction, wearing a shirt that was much too tight. She rolled her eyes and focused on the clear waters near her feet.

"Talking to yourself now?" Bryant took a seat on the grassy floor at her side, not bothering to ask for permission.

Whitleigh huffed.

"I knew wedding planning would send you over the edge."

She dismissed his remark with a scowl. "Where are Reese and Lennon?"

"Inside with your momma. *Petit fours* baking practice." He wiggled his fingers, mimicking their excitement. "Crazy wedding stuff." He waved at the air. "Blaine's helping your Dad. I think he's trying to impress Lennon."

"Tell him good luck with that." Whitleigh hid a grin in the nook of her elbow. "Shouldn't you be helping them too?"

"Thought I'd come say 'hi' first." He bumped her shoulder with his. "Besides, I'm not Professor Rhine's favorite person, if you know what I mean."

True. "Who could forget the classroom showdown?" Whitleigh stroked her forearm. "He's forgiving."

Bryant didn't contend. No need.

"What about you, Whit-bit?" He poked at her side. Whitleigh scoffed at the nickname. "Maybe you should go help the girls make petit fours?" He rubbed at his stomach. "I'm willing to taste as many as I need to. I'm here to make sure your wedding guests have only the best quality desserts."

"Sure you are."

"Oh, I get it. You want to bask in my presence." Bryant

pulled Whitleigh into his arms in a giant bear hug. "Get on up there before I have to turn my charm on full throttle. You'll never be able to resist me then."

"Not in the mood." Whitleigh struggled within his grasp.

"Hey. You crying, Whit?"

"No." Whitleigh dabbed her face with the neck of her T-shirt.

Bryant loosened his hold and draped an arm around Whitleigh's neck. She sank forward under the weight. "I'm listening."

"You listened better before you started hitting on me all the time." She sniffled. "Puberty ruined our friendship."

"Ha. It was that kiss, wasn't it? Give me a do-over. One more."

Whitleigh managed a short laugh through a stuffy nose. Her toes dug deeper into the mud. "You should ask Reese out. I think she'd keep you in line."

"Nah." Bryant's mouth curved downward. "I'm too much man for her to handle."

"You're probably right." Reese would manhandle him.

"Talk, Whit." Bryant plucked a blade of grass from the ground.

"Relationship issues."

"Ah. Well, in that case, I can tune you out and do a really good job of pretending to listen."

They took turns tossing pebbles into the river. Whitleigh counted the generations of ripples beyond the initial impact of the rock. A turtle peeped its head through the rings of water, disrupting her count.

Bryant sighed, breaking the silence. "Okay. Seriously. You

think you guys are gonna work it out?"

Whitleigh gave a half shrug.

"As much as I love you, and I do, you know, you and Collier are good together." He groaned, tossing a blade of grass aside, face growing more serious than she'd ever seen.

Whitleigh winced. "You're admitting this? Out loud?"

"I've seen the two of you together, and you're better together than apart."

"That's the problem." Whitleigh tucked the corner of her bottom lip beneath her teeth. "He's going to be gone for a year in Korea. I can't go with him." She rocked on her tailbone. "I've dropped everything to be with him. School. My scholarship. Cashed out my savings to help cover the wedding costs. For what? To not be with him?"

Bryant nodded. He tossed a small pebble. It sank beneath the water, leaving a ring of ripples behind. "You're wondering if you want to marry him now. Cold feet? That why you jammed them in that mud?"

"No." Whitleigh sighed, rolling her neck. "Maybe. Go away Bryant." She shoved his arm from her neck. "I don't need you trying to swoop in."

Bryant watched the water for a moment. Whitleigh tried but couldn't quite figure out his expression. "Tell me this." He rested a hand on his knee. "And tell me the truth. Do you love him?"

"That's silly, Bryant."

"Then what's the issue?" He lifted a shoulder to his ear. "If saying yes was right when things were going as planned, then why wouldn't it still be right when something gets in your way?"

"I don't know. Because." She slapped at his arm. "Nothing about this marriage has gone according to plan."

"Doesn't sound like the Whit I know. Where's your faith?"

"I've been asked that way too many times," Whitleigh grumbled, holding her head in the palm of her hands. Where was her faith? "I thought I had it, or found it. Now?" She sighed into her hands. "I don't know." Could she trust God now? "When did you get so wise anyway?"

"I listen in church too, you know."

Whitleigh cracked a smile. She exhaled, shaking her head. "So what do I do?"

"That's up to you." Bryant blew out his cheeks. "If you choose not to marry him…" He ran a shaking hand over the back of his head. "Well, I'm here, Whit."

His green eyes, much different from Collier's twin pools of blue, met hers. He placed a hand over hers, leaning forward.

Whitleigh swallowed. She scooted sideways, opening up more space between them.

Bryant clenched his jaw, turning away for a split moment. "Why didn't we work out, Whit? What did I do wrong?"

"Come on Bryant. We've been over this." Whitleigh smirked, pushing at his shoulder.

"I'm serious. What does Collier have that I don't?"

Her smile dissolved. She combed her hands along the length of her braid. How to answer?

"You know he's enlisted, right? I'll be an officer when I graduate. I can give you more." Bryant kicked at the riverbank with the heel of his leather boots.

"The fact you think that would make any difference is one good reason why we didn't work out. I don't care about what he can or can't financially provide." Whitleigh narrowed her eyes. "You can't buy me. You can't make me fall in love with how amazing you think you are. I'm not impressed."

"So maybe if I dropped out of school and left you behind like Collier, then you'd be ready to marry me at the drop of a hat. I guess I was just too good to you, too nice and considerate."

"You're such a jerk." Whitleigh jumped to her feet and lost her balance. She flailed her arms, but continued to fall back. The tip of her hair skimmed the surface of the river just as Bryant lunged forward, catching her in his arms. He pulled her close to his body and pressed his lips to hers.

Whitleigh pried her hands between their faces. She stumbled back and glared at him through the narrowed slits of her eyes. As if by instinct, her hand rose and collided against his jaw with a resounding crack. A sharp pain shot up her arm. Bryant stood perfectly still, unmoved and unmoving, while a red welt the shape and size of her hand formed on his face. Whitleigh yanked a handful of grass and pebbles from the ground and launched it in his direction.

He didn't bother to dodge the projectiles. "If you give me a chance—"

"You don't love me, Bryant." She scrubbed at her lips.

He winced. Whitleigh stood her ground. "You love the fact I'm the only girl that's never given in to you. I'm not a game."

"Whit—"

"Stop." Whitleigh stomped the ground, dismissing the pointed rocks boring into her feet. She swept her boots from the riverbank and held them in a white-knuckled grasp. A cough escaped her throat and she choked on words better left unspoken. Her head throbbed faster than her beating heart. A longtime cherished relationship ended today with an unwarranted kiss. Would another end as well? If only Collier were here to help her make a decision for their future.

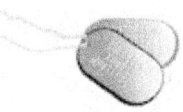

WHITLEIGH tied the apron around her waist. Her hands trembled. She dragged her palms over a wadded dish towel to wipe away the dampness. She dared not lick her lips. She'd scoured them to the point of raw with bare hands, forearms, and the fabric of her shirt.

"He kissed you? Just now? For real?" Lennon held the icing bowl on her hip, mouth gaping open. Her oversized Periodic Table shirt puffed out the side of her apron. "What kind of kiss?"

"Where's he at?" Reese slammed a batter covered spatula into the dishwater with a sudsy splash. The multi-colored beads draped around her neck swung like a pendulum. "Who does he think he is forcing you to kiss him?"

"My arm still hurts." Whitleigh's cheeks grew hot. She rubbed at her arm, and then folded them. Her muscles tensed. "I should've kicked him in the groin."

"What is Collier going to say?" Lennon's words squeaked out.

Whitleigh groaned. "I don't even know if we're getting married now."

"What?" Lennon dropped the mixing bowl. Icing splattered on the checkered tile floor.

Reese's eyes bulged. A strange squawk escaped between her pouting lips.

"Everyone calm down." Momma pulled a sheet pan from the refrigerator, placed it on the counter, and took a seat at the old round kitchen table. "Whit, honey, sit down."

Whitleigh took a seat at the table, shoulders pressed to the back of the chair.

"The wedding is six weeks away." Momma covered Whitleigh's hands with her own. Warm and gentle. Those were Momma's hands. "You can't call the wedding off based on

Bryant's grab for your affection."

"For real." Reese and Lennon bobbed their heads in unison.

"There's more. Much more." Whitleigh lifted a spoon from the table and dug into the mixing bowl in the center. She scooped up a hunk of pink icing and shoveled it into her mouth. This conversation called for a lot of sugar. "Got any milk?"

Lennon poured glasses of milk for each person at the table. Whitleigh talked, filling them in on the details of the day. Momma sat silent, while Reese and Lennon gasped and groaned.

After several minutes and many petit fours later, Whitleigh slouched forward, sipping at the last bit of milk in her cup. "So that's the whole story." She propped her chin on a balled fist. Her eyes watered a tad. "I don't know if I can trust God. I know He said yes about marrying Collier, but now things are different."

"Maybe the situation has changed, but God hasn't."

"Ugh. That's what Bryant said."

Momma crossed her legs. "You can't let fear stop you from doing what God wants you to do."

Whitleigh bowed her head. Momma was right, but it didn't make the situation any easier. "I don't know what to do. I don't know if I can marry Collier."

The timer on the oven buzzed. No one moved to remove the contents.

"Um, I'll get that." Whitleigh stood, retrieved the thin layer of sheet cake, and placed it on the cooling rack next to the stove.

"Do you love Bryant?" Momma leaned into her chair.

"No." Whitleigh flicked her wrist. "Yes, as a friend." She closed the oven door with her hip. "He's like a brother."

Reese and Lennon exchanged sighs. "You had me worried for a second, Whit." Lennon fanned her face. She straightened out her apron.

"Collier said he'd understand if I couldn't go through with the wedding, or stay with him." The words strangled her heart. She lowered her head and scooped a warm piece of cake from the tray. It crumbled in her hand. "Maybe all these setbacks are God's way of saying Collier and I aren't meant to be."

"If you think that, Whit, then I haven't raised you right."

"Momma."

"If God told you to do something that doesn't mean it's going to be easy or that you won't have setbacks. You persevere."

Reese and Lennon sat quietly on the edges of their seats.

"This is so much bigger than persevering Momma, and it's bigger than what man I should choose to marry." Whitleigh nibbled on a cake crumb and wrung her hands clean. "What kind of life am I signing up for? How can I teach and do summer missions with him going away for a year at a time and me worried for his safety?"

"You think you need a classroom to teach and an overseas destination to do missions? You teach by the way you live. Your mission field is all around you. Can't you see that? God wants you to love Him and others, whether or not you ever marry or who you decide to marry."

Whitleigh couldn't make eye contact with her momma. Momma's words made it difficult for Whitleigh to even lift her head. Truth hurts. Truth stings.

Reese and Lennon remained quiet. Whitleigh refused to let a tear fall. She'd cried enough today.

Momma scooted the chair from the table. Her arm draped across Whitleigh and pulled her close. "Collier is following God's calling. Do you think it would make him any safer if he were to stay here with you? We aren't called to an easy life,

Whit, but an obedient life."

"What's so wrong with what I have planned?" Tears beaded in the corner of her eyes. "It's all good things." Whitleigh laid her head on Momma's shoulder and closed her eyes.

"You've got a big heart, sweet girl, and all the things you want to do are good... they're great, but God wants the best for you, not good or great." Momma kissed her forehead and continued. "Doing what God wants you to do may never be fun or easy, but it's where you're gonna find joy and peace. That's what you want baby. You don't want things to go your way, or for all your plans to go accordingly, not really anyway. It's joy and peace you want."

She lifted Whitleigh's chin until their eyes met. Momma's eyes sparkled. "Now you need to decide what it is God wants you to do so you can snatch that joy and peace right up."

Whitleigh gave a short smile. She knew the answer, right? Joy and peace—yeah, that sounded nice. Definitely something she needed right now, but what to decide? Was she even supposed to get married? Her head ached.

"Why don't we pray about this, Whit?" Momma folded her hands in her lap. "This is a tough situation. No answer is pretty for anyone involved." Momma patted her lap. Her knees jostled to and fro. She did that when fighting off tears.

"Here." Reese extended her hands. Lennon locked hands with Reese and Momma.

Whitleigh took hold and finished forming the circle around the kitchen table where more than meals were shared. "I'll start."

ZEALOUS children filled the halls, biting at the bit for summer vacation to begin. Their sneakers squeaked across the tile floor as they made their way to and from lunch, singing as they ambled along. The teachers, as weary as most looked, joined in the celebration. One last hurrah.

Whitleigh stood close to the classroom doorway and high fived the kiddos as they passed. Up high, down low, too fast, too slow. Forcing herself to laugh wasn't hard around them. They lifted her spirits and provided that joy and peace while she waited for God to provide an answer. Marry Collier or not? If not now, when? Or ever?

"Come on in Mrs. Ruther's class." Whitleigh patted their backs as they filed in. She counted heads and faces. Still no Brady. He never missed and wasn't one to be tardy. "Alright kiddos. Mrs. Ruthers will be back in a sec. Put your lunch stuff away and let's line up at the door for recess."

Most of the children sprang into action. "Careful. Watch where you're going." A few of them butted heads.

"Now is it time for the water balloon fight?" Jameson folded his arms as he stood.

A few of the pigtailed girls answered before Whitleigh had the chance. "Stop asking or we'll never get to it."

"Let's speak nicely." Whitleigh hid her smile as she glanced toward the doorway.

Mrs. Ruthers hurried down the hall. Her facial features downturned. "Go ahead and take them out. I'll be right there."

"Everything okay?"

"I'll fill you in."

Whitleigh wrinkled her brow. "Um. Ok."

Mrs. Ruthers moved down the hall toward the principal's office without further explanation.

Whitleigh led the children down the hall, to the right, and out the side doors toward the playground. Sunlight greeted them as they stepped outside. Jameson ran after squealing girls.

Others sat in the sandbox and pushed cars along dirt paths. One or two flung themselves wildly across the monkey bars. Some resorted to the swings. Their small feet swung high into the air and looked strange compared to the giant sky overhead. All of these children were fearless. Fearless to a fault, yet, wasn't that faith? Whitleigh smiled. A childlike faith, yes, she wanted that.

"Ms. Haynes." Mrs. Ruthers called from the double doors, waving her over. She stood with the principal.

Whitleigh hugged her arms to her chest. Apparently something was up.

"Ms. Haynes." The principal's brows drew together. Her graying hair appeared unusually untidy. "We know you're close to Brady."

Whitleigh's lips parted. Her heart stopped.

Mrs. Ruthers reached for Whitleigh's hand. "He's okay, Whitleigh."

Whitleigh slumped over, holding her knees. "Thank God."

The principal placed a hand on her shoulder. "His daddy's been hurt. They don't think he's going to make it overnight. Brady's with his family right now waiting to hear news."

Oh, Brady. No. Whitleigh shook her head in mute denial. Did she dare ask? "Wha… what happened?"

"The insurgents in Iraq set off a roadside bomb as his father's convoy passed." The principal lowered her head for a moment. She wiped a tear. "Most of the men were killed."

Whitleigh worked to breathe past the tightening sensation growing in her chest. "Can I see Brady?"

"We hoped you'd ask." Mrs. Ruthers exchanged a glance with the principal. "His Momma said he's been asking for you to come. He says you'll pray for his dad… and…" she choked a bit and swiped at the tears falling from her eyes, "… and he'll get better."

"Give me an address and I'm there." Whitleigh took the slip of paper from the principal's hand and made her way to the car. No time remained to doubt, only act.

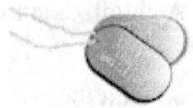

MAY 22nd

Dear Collier,

Collier sat outside his barrack. It had been too long since a letter came from Whit. His stomach knotted as his eyes scanned over her words.

Where do I start?

So much has happened. I've spent a lot of time since we last talked praying about what I should do.

I've doubted, I've worried, I've pouted, I've been kissed by Bryant, and forced to question if I really loved you, wanted to marry you now, or ever.

What? Collier clenched his jaw. Bryant went too far. Collier's heartbeat pounded in his ears.

I've concluded that none of it matters.

Didn't matter? Collier bit at his thumbnail.

Not that you don't matter or we don't matter, but as I sit here beside Brady, this sweet boy whose dad—a soldier—was injured and now fighting for his life, I have a new perspective. Life is fleeting, and what am I if I'm not loving God and loving others?

I have to honestly say that I'm still unsure about what answer to give you, but I am praying about it. I will not leave you hanging. I will not let you leave for Korea without an answer. Please forgive me for putting you through this, and I can understand if you are angry with me, but I want peace and joy, and that comes from obeying God, and not through following any of my own desires. Can you understand that?

He understood it more than most things in life. Collier gripped his chin. Whit made sense. He got it, but still, the waiting was killer. What if she said no? Did it change his decision to be obedient to what God called him to do? Collier huffed. Of course it didn't change his path, only made it more difficult.

I want to make sure I'm really obeying God.

Collier pinched the bridge of his nose, head bowed. This is what he'd prayed for Whit—to be fearless, follow God no matter what. She's just looking for assurance before she takes that leap, but where would she leap? The letter shook in Collier's hand. He gripped his chin and smiled through the pain in his heart. No matter where Whit decided to leap, he'd be happy and certain it was in the direction God wanted her to go.

I won't see you until your graduation... do you want to hear my decision then?

Maybe. Collier shook his head. He'd want to see her no matter what she'd have to say.

Please know I love you. So much. More than myself, my plans, your plans, any of our wants or desires.
Love me always,
Whit

Collier held the letter over his heart. "I'll always love you Whit."

He pulled out a small notepad and began to write.

Dear Whit,

~~Bryant kissed you? I'm gonna~~

~~I know you're going through a lot. I'm so sorry...~~

~~I miss you. I love you. Take your time deciding~~

Forget it. Collier crumbled the paper and shoved it into his uniform pocket. He tugged on his dog tags as he rose to his feet. The phone booth line would be shorter this time of day anyway.

The phone rang only once.

"Whit?"

"Collier." Her voice carried waves of relief through loud music and clanging dishes. "Hold on a sec. I'll take my break. It's so good to hear your voice."

"It's always good to hear yours." He smiled like she could see.

"I'm guessing you got my letter." The background noise faded.

"It's always good getting something from you." He pressed the receiver close to his mouth. So much to say. So much not to say.

"You mad?"

"At Bryant."

"Ignore him." She scoffed. "I put him in his place. He's still pretty sore over it."

"I bet."

Neither said much. Collier raked his teeth over his bottom lip. Afternoon sunlight lit up the phone booth like a magnifying glass—he was the ant.

"Brady's dad?" Collier rubbed a hand over the back of his neck.

"Still not looking good." She made a clicking noise. "Brady's hanging in there and so is his momma. The church has stepped in to help with meals and housework. It's amazing to see really."

"Haden and I will pray for Brady's dad and his family."

"Prayers work."

The silence returned.

"I know you worry about me going to war, Whit. I can't promise—"

"Collier, you don't have to promise or explain."

"So, um." He tucked a hand in the back pocket of his uniform. "I've been thinking about the Honduras trip." Not really, but it gave them something to talk about other than one of many depressing topics.

"You gonna be able to go?"

Maybe he should've picked another subject. He shook his head. "Um, I, well, I'm sure there's someone else who can go." Silently he added, *just not Bryant.*

"I understand." Her voice didn't sound understanding. "I'm sure the name on the plane ticket can still be switched out."

"So you're still going?"

"Is that a bad thing?"

"I want you to go. It'll be good." Collier smacked his forehead. He pressed his lips together. Why couldn't he say what he wanted? Beg her to marry him? No. He wouldn't. She needed this time to think and pray.

"I know waiting for me to give you an answer is torture." She sighed. "I'm so sorry Collier. I'm not trying to hurt you."

"I love you, Whit." He let his shoulders drop. "I'll wait for your answer and be okay with your decision... even if..." his throat dried. "Even if it's not what I want." He pressed a palm to the glass window of the phone booth. The drill sergeant would make him clean the prints off later. "Above my happiness, or what I want, I want you to follow God." He sighed. At times the truth was heavy. "You're right about finding peace and joy in obeying God."

"You've got it, don't you?"

He smirked. "Through it all." Collier held a hand over his heart. "Through it all."

"Collier?"

"You gotta get back to work?"

"Tables waiting."

"Sounds like the tables are turning on this conversation."

"Ha."

"I'm the one who usually has to go."

"I love you, Collier."

"I love you more than myself, Whit. Always and forever." He closed his eyes. "So I'll see you at the graduation ceremony."

"I wouldn't miss it. I know I'll have an answer for you by then."

His heart pounded in his chest.

"See ya." Her voice rose with a slight giggle.

The line went dead. Collier held the phone in his hand for a moment and then hung it on the receiver. He stepped from the booth and lifted his chin toward the sky. Trusting and waiting—not matter what.

JUNE 16th

COLLIER stood in the position of attention. Well-manicured green grass bent beneath his shiny black shoes. Second in formation, third row back, dead center, Haden at his right side on the ceremony field. Collier's knees bent at a slight angle. Soldiers who locked their knees in formation passed out, a strange yet entertaining sight to behold. He squinted, rubbing the blue nylon cord dangling from his hand. The Georgia sun glared and beat down on the bleachers overflowing with anxious family and friends. Whit sat amongst the crowd. Somewhere.

Collier's Adam's apple dropped and caught on the collar of his dress uniform. Beads of sweat bubbled on the small of his back. She'd have an answer for him today.

"We made it." Haden's voice rolled out in a low whisper. "Can you believe we made it?"

"I wouldn't believe it if you didn't." Collier gave a slight nod in Haden's direction. Haden stood, chest puffed out, alongside the other soldiers. Collier smiled and looked forward.

"You got it with you?" Haden all but winked.

Collier's cheeks warmed. "Right here." He tapped his side pants pocket.

"Good man. It'll work out, you'll see."

Hopefully. Collier swallowed and tapped the small box tucked into his pocket. His hands dampened and he pushed the box, the ring, and a possible proposal from his mind.

The Commander of Ceremony took his place at the podium, first turning to the audience of civilians. "Family, friends, welcome to the Turning Blue Ceremony." He then positioned himself in front of the newbie soldiers, back turned to the crowd. "Infantrymen, you have set yourselves apart from other soldiers of the armed forces merely by your appearance. You are stronger, faster, highly trained, always prepared, and deadlier than any weapon."

Collier stood tall. Muscles, now much larger than those fourteen weeks prior to Basic, flexed beneath the jacket of his Army greens. His buttoned uniform stretched taut across his chest.

The Commander of Ceremony surveyed the soldiers before him. "You, Infantrymen, are the only branch of service that holds this blue cord. Ever since the Civil War, Infantrymen have worn blue to signify courage and honor."

Everything God called him to in life, in love. Collier took an inward breath, letting it fill his chest.

"You, Infantrymen, are not called to a life of comfort. You will find yourselves hungry, tired, and wet, but never alone. The men to your right and left serve and sacrifice with you. These fine few and proud are your brothers."

Collier and the other soldiers in formation bent their arms into a salute, responding to the Commander of Ceremony. The tips of his fingers hovered at the edge of his brow. He held the salute until the Commander dropped his.

"Parade rest." The Commander's voice echoed over the expanse of the field. The soldiers thudded into position in a single swift motion, legs shoulder length apart, back of their hands pressed to the small of their backs. "Family and friends, you may now turn your soldier blue. Please place the cord over their right shoulder."

The bleachers emptied. He waited, silent, alongside Haden. Would Whit show? Of course. She had an answer to give and he prayerfully hoped it was one he wanted to hear. Collier tugged at his collar. Too much remained unsaid between them for her not to come.

Haden whistled the Army song and tapped his toe, waiting for no one in particular. Making the trip from Oregon to Georgia would've financially crippled his family.

Collier buried his mouth on top his clutched fist. His gaze landed on family members gathered around their soldier, helping to place the infantry cord on their son's shoulder. His mom would've been here. So would his brother. Collier gave a nod to Heaven. Whether they could look down on him now, he didn't know, but he found comfort in the thought.

Collier cleared his throat as it tightened. "Want me to give you a hand with the cord, Haden?"

"Haden?" A delicate voice called from the crowd.

Haden's posture stiffened. His lips parted. "Emilee."

She leapt into his wide embrace.

"I can't believe you came!" He swung her side to side. "Kiss me."

Collier tried not to watch or listen, but their glee splattered into his personal space. He huffed and folded his arms, averting his gaze.

There. She was almost hidden by people much taller than she. Collier stood on the balls of his feet. There, again. Long, blonde hair brushing against her shoulders. A whimsical floral dress gathered at the waist. Large sunglasses covering those sparkling blue eyes. Whit. His heart sighed. She came, like she said she would.

One leg in front of the other, her hips swayed until she stood inches from him. She pulled her sunglasses off, closing them in her hands. Her red lips curved upward. Beautiful. He remembered to breathe.

"You're here." He reached out, cradling her elbows in his palm.

"I said I would be."

"I thought with everything that happened between us, well, you know." He winced. "I thought you might change your mind about coming."

Her lips folded into a pout. "I'll always be there for you."

He wrapped her in his arms, fingers tangled in the hair

spilled down her back. It hurt so good to hold her. "I've got so much I want to say."

"Right now, let me turn you blue." She giggled, hand held out. Collier placed the cord in her palm.

"Am I doing this right?" She tugged at the buttoned shoulder tab on his dress jacket.

He nodded his head. Her touch rendered him silent.

With a careful pat of the shoulder tab, she finished. The blue braided infantry cord hung over and under his right shoulder, officially making him a warrior; one of America's finest.

"Whit?" Collier wet his lips, collecting her hands in his. He leaned forward. Did he dare steal a kiss? She didn't move.

"I won't keep you waiting any longer." Her eyes searched his. "If you'll still have me, I'd love to be your wife." No hesitation existed in her voice.

Collier fought the urge to shout and twirl her all at once. "Are you sure?" He held her face between his hands.

She nodded and laughed. Her eyes sparkled.

"This isn't going to be easy for either of us." He released his hold on her face and brushed his palm across her smooth cheek. "You heard the Commander speaking, and we're both getting a taste of all the uncertainties in the Army."

"I'd rather face life's battles as your wife than as your girlfriend." Those words were a melody.

He heard it with his own ears. Letters and phone calls couldn't compare to hearing the words first hand.

"What about all the plans you've made for your future? What about summer mission trips? Who's going to go on the mission trip in my place?" Why did he care? She said yes.

"Now who's having doubts?"

"No doubts. Not ever. I only want to make sure that you're sure."

Whit chuckled. Her hair shimmered in the sunlight. "If it tells you anything, I threw away my calendar."

"No."

"Yup." She pressed her lips together and arched a brow. "Reese and Lennon said it was time for an intervention. Ha. They were right, so we got out the calendar, ripped it to shreds, and decided I could have one again when I stopped relying so heavily on it."

"Wow."

"And why would I only do summer mission trips when my mission field is anywhere I go?"

"You're incredible."

"I'm so thankful God helped me to see these things. He's given me amazing friends and family to pray with me and give sound advice." She radiated peace and joy. Collier stepped back only a bit and admired her. She pulled him close. "As far as the Honduras trip goes…" Her grin slid sideways. "I've got a plan for your replacement."

Collier winced.

"It's not Bryant." She tilted her head and placed a hand on her hip.

How could he not appear relieved? Collier slowly bobbed his head. "I'm a bit sore over him kissing you."

Whit tucked her chin. Her shoulders sank. "I didn't want that to—"

"Not at you, but a bit at him still." Collier gathered Whit into his arms. "I'm more upset that he was the last one to kiss you."

The sly grin returned to her face. "Want to change that?"

Collier lifted Whitleigh from the ground. She giggled, arms tight around his neck. He placed her feet back on the ground and covered her face with kisses. The sweet scent of sweet pea and honeysuckle that defined her so well swirled around him.

Collier removed a small box from the pocket of his dress pants. He lifted Whitleigh's hand as he took a knee. Whitleigh covered her mouth. Her eyes glistened.

"You deserve a proper proposal." He slid the piece of parachute cord from her left ring finger. "You deserve a proper ring." Collier removed the solitaire diamond ring from its case. "Whitleigh Haynes, would you do me the great honor of becoming my wife?"

"Yes."

He stood. "You won't regret this, Whitleigh Haynes." He kissed her once more, holding her face between his palms. She pressed her forehead into his chest, arms tight around his back.

"Congratulations." Haden's deep voice roared around them.

Collier laughed out loud. "Hey, Whit. I want you to meet Haden, my best man, and this is his girlfriend, Emilee."

Collier watched Whit light up as she shook hands. Whit, his fiancé, his soon to be wife.

CHAPTER 9

WHITLEIGH inhaled and glanced around her childhood bedroom for the last time as Whitleigh Haynes. The sweet, subtle scent of lavender and lilac drifted past lace curtains and danced under her nose. She smiled.

Whitleigh stole a glimpse of herself in the full length oval mirror her father had hung in the room's corner after her sixth birthday. Small round pearls dangled from her wrist—a prized piece once worn by Collier's mother.

"You look stunning." Momma placed her hand on Whitleigh's cheek with care. "Raising children happens so fast. One day you're in the thick of parenting and, before you know it, you are staring at them — the end product, thinking how amazing the journey has been and what an honor it is to just have played a part in their lives." Momma sniffled past her soft smile. "I could not be more proud of the godly woman that you are. I love you."

"I love you, too, Momma."

Lennon grabbed boxes of tissues and passed them to Reese, both of them looked stunning in their deep purple bridesmaids' dresses.

"Knock, knock." Dad entered with covered eyes.

"We're decent, Daddy."

Professor Rhine stood at his side, envelope in hand, ponytail tied with a more festive ribbon.

Daddy stopped in front of Whitleigh. He clasped his hands, eyes sparkling. "You took my breath away."

Whitleigh bowed her head, feeling the heat in her cheeks. She held on to his hand lightly, swinging their arms. "You're not so bad all dressed up in a tux."

He fiddled with the black bow tie. "Collier looks pretty sharp out there, so I'm trying not to show him up."

Momma laughed along. Reese and Lennon sat on the bedside, still holding tissues to their eyes.

"It's about time to start." Dad tugged on the cuffs of his sleeve. "Julius has something to give you."

Professor Rhine stepped forward, envelope held out in his wrinkled hand. "After Korea, Collier will get first pick of duty stations." His sanguine eyes held her attention. "Being former military, I've acquired many properties."

He slipped the envelope into Whitleigh's hands. Her brows met in the middle as she turned the card over. A key fell from the corner and into her palm. "I don't understand."

"Go to school in Colorado. Live in one of my apartments until Collier gets orders to Ft. Carson, and then you can move on base if you'd like. The Army will move your stuff once he has orders there."

Whitleigh's voice caught. "I... I don't know what to say." She held a hand over her heart.

"I held you and Collier as babies. Fought in the Korean War with his grandfather and yours." He lifted his hands, palms open. "This is the least I can do."

Thank you seemed insufficient. Professor Rhine squeezed Whitleigh's wrist and walked to the door. "And that doesn't mean I'm giving either of you an A." He winked and headed out.

Momma held tight to Daddy. Both their chins dimpled.

Reese and Lennon no longer hid their sobs.

"It's time, Whit." Daddy tapped at his pocket watch.

Whitleigh parted her lips, still in awe of the generosity of all those around her. She lifted her bouquet. Lavender buds and pearls skimmed the top of her hand. Lace and burlap tickled her skin. "One more thing."

She lifted the corner of her dress, maneuvering across her bedroom. "Lennon." Whitleigh knelt as much as her dress would allow. "Collier won't be going to Honduras next month."

"But —"

"Wait." Whitleigh bit at her lip. "We want you to go in his place."

"Whit, there's no way I can afford —"

"It's already paid for." Her lashes danced across the top of her cheeks. "Don't argue." Whitleigh held up a playful hand. "Just say yes."

Lennon's cheeks rounded. Her grin matched the width of her face. "Blaine's going, too."

"I knew it. You like him." Reese slung her lanky arms around both Whitleigh and Lennon. "Best day ever."

"Remember the scar or you could end up kissing Bryant."

"Ick!" Lennon and Reese laughed to the point of doubling over.

"Honduras here we come!" Whitleigh clapped her hands.

"Let's get you married first." Momma dabbed at her eyes and patted Whitleigh's hand. Yes, it was time to get married. Finally.

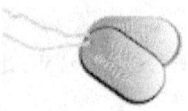

THOSE standing in reverence blocked the view of her groom. Soft music floated through the rafters. Early afternoon sunlight cascaded through barn-wood slats, more spectacular than the glistening of a thousand diamonds. This was no longer a barn, but a holy place for a holy occasion. Fragrant floral arrangements embellished with small iridescent sparkling butterflies, signifying new life, adorned the wooden chairs lining the aisle.

A crown of crystals adorned her hair. Layers of elegant white satin and chiffon kissed the ground beneath her feet. Whitleigh closed the distance between her and Collier. The crowd vanished. Through her veil she could see him — the man God made for her. The medals on his chest shone in the dim light as he stood tall and proud in his Army Greens.

Daddy placed her hand into Collier's and stepped aside. Collier held her hands. His thumbs rubbed smooth circles overtop hers. He not only held her hands, he held her heart.

The pastor opened his worn Bible and the ceremony began.

"Marriage is sacred, created and designed by God. We witness God's outline for marriage in Genesis chapter two when Eve was created." The pastor's nimble fingers flipped the tattered pages. "This is now bone of my bones, and flesh of my flesh; she shall be called Woman, because she was taken out of Man. For this reason, a man shall leave his father and his mother, and be joined to his wife; and they shall become one flesh.

She refused to take her eyes from Collier's. They beckoned her.

The pastor balanced the Bible with one hand. "The marriage union is the closest relationship that can exist between two people. It should not be entered into lightly. Rings please."

Collier shifted his weight and wiped the sweat from his brow. His hand trembled as he slid the ring onto her finger with ease.

"Do you, Collier Cromwell, take Whitleigh Haynes as your lawfully wedded wife from this day forward, keeping yourself only unto her, for richer or for poorer, in sickness and in health, until death do you part?"

Collier squeezed Whit's hand. "I do."

She returned the gesture.

"Do you, Whitleigh Haynes, take Collier Cromwell to be your lawfully wedded husband from this day forward, keeping yourself only unto him, for richer or for poorer, in sickness and in health, until death do you part?"

"I do." Whitleigh touched the ring she placed on her husband's hand. Hands much larger than hers. Stronger. A place where her hands belonged.

"I now pronounce you man and wife."

Their audience clapped and cheered.

The pastor snapped his Bible shut. "You may kiss your bride."

And kiss they did.

WHITLEIGH breathed in the moment and all the setting offered to her senses. Long family sized farm tables sat in parallel rows through the freshly mowed field behind the barn. Each table boasted wooden slab centerpieces smelling of fresh maple. Mason jars perched on top of the wood pieces with lilac and lavender sprouting from them. Burlap and lace runners hung from the sides. The beautiful blue sky provided a picturesque backdrop for the wedding reception.

Family and friends raved about the paracord bracelet wedding favors. Laughter and chatter surrounded Whitleigh and Collier as they danced, bodies close. The heat from his skin warmed her bare shoulders. He kissed the nape of her neck and spun her around.

"Your dance moves have improved." She chuckled.

"Let's just say that my basic training buddies may or may not have taught me a few things."

"Now that's a funny sight, a bunch of grown men — Army men — teaching each other to dance."

Collier grinned. "It may or may not have happened. Ha, look at my buddies over there." He nodded with his head, and then spun her twice. A breeze carried the scents the potato bar's many succulent toppings past her nose. Her stomach growled. She eyed the buffet table. Bryant stood, shirt untucked, hands in his pocket.

He waved and started in their direction.

Her stomach lurched, and she stilled in Collier's embrace.

"What's wrong?" The wrinkles on Collier's forehead folded on top of each other.

Whitleigh simply stared.

"Oh." Collier placed himself in front of Whitleigh. She sighed, grateful. "I'll handle this."

Bryant held his hands out, palms facing the sky. "I'm not here to start anything."

"You were way out of line, Bryant." Collier tightened his fist. Haden walked over, placing a hand on Collier's shoulder, but remained silent.

"I wanted to apologize to you and to Whit." He huffed, his hand falling from the back of his neck. "I should've never done what I did."

"That's right. We were friends, Bryant."

Bryant nodded. "We've all been friends a long time. I'm not expecting an overnight fix, but in time, I'd like to think we can move past what I did."

He seemed sincere. Whitleigh hung her arm through Collier's, working to loosen his tense muscles. Whitleigh nodded. "In time, Bryant."

"That's all I'm asking." He grinned, but only for a moment. "May I talk with you Whit? In private?"

"Is this a joke?" Collier stepped between Bryant and Whit.

Whitleigh held Collier's hand. Haden still hung close by. "It's okay, Collier. I'll talk with him, but we'll stay out here for everyone to see."

"That's fair." Bryant nodded.

Whitleigh watched Collier pop his knuckles. He swung his arms at his side.

"I'm okay Collier." She kissed his cheek and he relaxed his stance.

Bryant extended a hand to Collier. Collier shook it, veins protruding on the back of his hand. Bryant pursed his lips and bowed out.

Haden laughed and swatted at Collier's shoulder. "Come hang out with me and Emms for a few minutes."

Whitleigh clutched the fabric of her dress and shuffled along by Bryant's side. She smiled and waved at friends and family as she passed. "The food table's far enough."

"That's fair." Bryant stopped and picked a grape from the table. He popped it in his mouth. "I've been thinking a lot about what you said to me."

"Oh." Whitleigh folded her arms. The sequins scratched her forearms.

"You're wrong about me not loving you—"

"C'mon Bryant, I'm married."

He held out a palm. "I do love you, as a friend, and you're right." He fidgeted with his fingers. "I've treated you like a challenge. I've done that with all the girls I've dated, or wanted to date, and I'm sorry."

No grin. No smirk. No winking. Bryant was serious. More serious than Whit had ever seen him. "I appreciate you saying that Bryant."

He gave a short nod and headed out.

"Please stay. Have fun." Whitleigh shrugged and offered a wide smile.

Bryant tossed another grape in his mouth. "I'm sure I can find something fun in the midst of all the lights and lace."

"Ha. I'm sure you can."

"Whit." Momma walked up. "Someone's here to see you."

"Everyone's here to see her, Ma'am." Bryant winked.

Whitleigh rolled her eyes and smiled as she followed behind Momma.

"Looks like you two are friends again."

"On our way." Whitleigh scooted past the food table, in front of the DJ, and through a crowd of family and friends. Her heels sank into the ground below her feet. "Where are we going?"

"Right. Here." Momma stopped beside the car lined driveway.

Brady hopped from a pint-sized minivan.

Whitleigh knelt and embraced the little boy. Her dress rustled beneath her as she lifted him up.

"Momma and Daddy are here too."

"What?" A miracle. Her heart swelled. Whitleigh held on to him. "Look at how handsome you are in your suit and tie."

"I'll go get Collier." Momma hurried toward the festivities.

Brady's mom slid from the driver's seat, opened up the sliding side door, and pulled out a wheelchair.

"Let me help." Whitleigh closed the space between them with one stride, Brady still very much attached to her. His mother accepted the offer with a kind smile.

The chair clanked into place and Brady's father slid from his seat into the wheelchair. Both legs were gone, but he was very much alive, and stronger than the last report. Whitleigh swallowed back her reservations.

"Mr. Jacobs, thank you for coming." How do you thank a man who's done so much for his family and country?

"We couldn't miss meeting the woman who prays with our little boy." He stretched out a hand. Whitleigh shook it and nodded. No words came.

"Thank you for all you've done, Ms. Haynes, I mean, Mrs. Cromwell." Brady's mother hugged her. "You are breathtaking."

"Thank you Mrs. Jacobs." Whitleigh's face warmed. She blinked back tears. "You guys are thanking me, but your son has a fierce faith that's helped me."

Collier joined Whitleigh at her side and slipped his arm around her waist. "I'm Collier. Thank you all for coming." He extended a hand to Brady's father. "Thank you for your service and sacrifice."

Mr. Jacobs nodded. They stared at one another for a

moment, not needing to speak, as if they both understood many things about service and sacrifice, or perhaps those things that were to come.

"We got you a gift," Brady chirped, his voice higher pitched than usual.

Mrs. Jacobs tugged a large frame from under the seat. "Psalm 91."

Whitleigh covered her mouth with the tips of her fingers.

"The soldier's prayer." Mr. Jacobs gripped the painting. He adjusted his weight in the wheelchair and winced.

"We prayed this for you, Daddy. Me and Ms. Haynes, I mean, Mrs. Cromwell."

"And we wanted the two of you to have it." Mrs. Jacob's didn't hide her tears. "Your prayers have meant the world to our family. God has blessed us with friends and family during this time in our lives."

She knew the feeling. Collier intertwined his fingers with hers.

"Please stay for a while. There's plenty of food." Collier gestured to the crowd. "I'm sure you'll feel right at home."

Brady jumped up and down, pleading.

"Just for a little bit, Brady." His momma smoothed down his hair. "Daddy needs to get plenty of rest."

Mr. Jacobs smiled. "Best part about this injury, lots of rest, and service with a smile." He tugged on his wife's arms, pulling her down for a kiss.

"Party's this way." Collier held the picture with one hand and Whitleigh's hand with the other. Brady grabbed at her free hand and she swung her arm with his.

Family and friends welcomed the Jacobs crew. Whitleigh watched Brady as he danced with Reese and Lennon. Professor

Rhine chatted with Mr. Jacobs. Oh, the Army stories Mr. Jacobs must be listening to. Poor guy.

Collier laughed and grabbed Whitleigh's elbow. "We better get away from here before we get caught up in a European history lecture."

"You don't see me arguing." Whitleigh placed her hand in Collier's. He led her toward the dance floor. "Dad outdid himself." Her heels click-clacked on the old barn wood.

Whitleigh lingered in Collier's arms. She nuzzled at his cheek. "We made it."

"We made it." Collier kissed the curve of her ear. They swayed to the sound of the wind as afternoon gave way to evening. Lightening bugs serenaded the dusk with their lights.

"Things are about to change." Whitleigh admired the glow of his skin in the faded daylight.

"They already have." The corner of his mouth lifted. "You scared?"

She drew in a deep breath, thoughtful of her response. "I guess I could be."

"But?"

"I don't know what my future holds, but I know who holds my future." Whitleigh looked up to heaven with a nod, and then kissed her soldier — her husband.

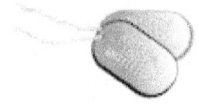

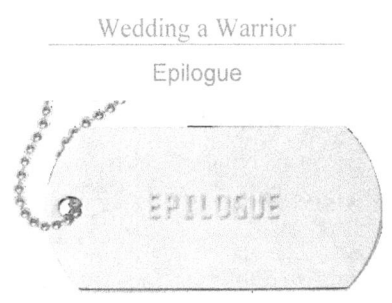

AND so it started—their last day. Whitleigh snuggled closer to Collier, her back buried into his chest. Heat radiated from his body and his chest rose and fell at a steady pace. She turned to her side, careful not to wake him. He had a long day ahead of him. So did she.

Whitleigh propped herself up with an elbow. If she could hold on to this moment, to all the other moments they shared, perhaps being apart would be easier. She traced his face with the tip of her finger. Across his forehead, over the sharp line of his nose, and along the slight arch of his dark brows. Dozens of freckles dotted his strong, squared shoulders. She snickered and touched each one. If she connected the dots, what picture would appear?

Collier stirred. Whitleigh leaned in and placed her lips on his.

"I felt you staring at me."

"How could I not?" She kissed him again.

"How did you sleep?" Collier rubbed sleep from his eyes.

"Not sure I did." Whitleigh reached for his hand and folded her fingers between his. "Sleeping wastes what little time we have together."

He didn't speak. No need. She knew his thoughts—they

were her own. Collier brushed her hair aside and kissed the nape of her neck. She'd miss that. Whitleigh closed her eyes.

"I dreamt we were in Niagara Falls." Collier tousled a lock of her hair. Whitleigh's body warmed. "Why are you blushing Mrs. Cromwell?"

"I'll never forget that trip as long as I live." What words existed to describe two becoming one? Intimate, mysterious, and beautiful don't quite measure up. Whitleigh sighed and cupped his face. "I hope you always dream of our honeymoon."

"We didn't see too much of the area though."

"I think we saw enough." Whitleigh cracked a smile. "I'm blushing at my own joke." She laughed and fell over him. He tickled her side.

"Thirty days went by too fast." Collier lowered his head. "I wish we had more time."

"More time would never be enough."

The alarm clock sounded. They fell silent. No tears right now. Whitleigh pushed back the burning in her throat. Her eyes welled. Not now. Not yet.

"Get dressed, Babes." Collier placed a quick peck on her cheek and rolled out of bed. "I'll get breakfast started."

Whitleigh followed suit. Her feet sank down into the plush carpet. Whitleigh stood and scanned their bedroom, the largest area in their apartment.

One photo from their wedding hung on the far wall closest to the dual closets. The other walls, tan and bare, begged to be filled. A few boxes from the move remained on their bedroom floor, but in all honesty, there's not much to move when two college kids get married.

Her heart pounded. The minutes ticked by on the clock perched on their nightstand. If she didn't move, time would freeze, right? Whitleigh swallowed and forced her feet forward.

Would it feel like this every time he left? Like her heart was being ripped out of her chest?

She dressed in their bathroom, mindful of her elbows in a space so tight. The old ankle-length skirt she purchased from the thrift store wasn't flattering, but was the required attire for women missionaries while in Honduras. Whitleigh leaned over the sink and peered into the mirror. A little makeup would help. She livened up her face with a bit of mascara and lip gloss, then headed down the stairs. Their suitcases, hers bulging, his a well-packed duffle bag, sat next to the front door.

Not much longer now. Whitleigh bobbed her head. She could do this. They could do this.

The scent of bacon greeted her. Collier stood in front of the stove and whistled a tune.

"Hey Babes." He turned, spatula in hand. "Well look at you, Senorita. Look out Honduras."

Whitleigh twirled and sent her skirt spinning. "You're not so bad yourself there, looking all nice in that uniform." She shimmied over in his direction. Worst Samba ever. She laughed and reached for the plate he held in his hand.

"Eggs over medium. Bacon well done."

"Perfect." Whitleigh sat down at their table for two. "Your cooking skills are impressive."

Collier took a bow and then the seat at her side. "I aim to please."

"You make it look easy."

"It's not that difficult to fry—"

"No." Whitleigh chuckled and snapped off a piece of bacon. "You make today look easy."

"Not easy." He shook his head and took a sip of juice. "Ready."

"Ready?"

"The sooner we get going, the sooner we can get back together." He winked and snuck in a kiss. "And I like together better than apart."

Whitleigh crunched the bacon between her teeth. She slid her arm into the nook of his elbow. "It's strange when you think about it—that we're starting our lives together, but literally worlds apart."

"God's got an interesting plan for us." He shuffled the eggs around his plate with a fork and scooped a few into his mouth. "A year's gonna fly by."

"I'm already saving to come see you—our first Christmas. Wow. I never thought it would be in Korea."

"I'm sure Reese and Lennon can come out here on breaks, and I know your mom and dad are already planning a trip."

"Two weeks." Whitleigh laid her head on his shoulder and gave it a squeeze. "School will start up soon too." So many changes. She smiled.

"Babes." Collier kissed the top of her head.

"It's time to go, isn't it?" She closed her eyes and held on to his arm with all her strength.

"Will you do something for me?"

Whitleigh lifted her chin. "Name it."

"The picture Brady and his family gave to us."

"Psalm 91?"

"Let's pray that scripture every day." He gathered her hands into his. "Could we do that?"

"Everyday." Praying for her husband was an honor.

"Can we pray it before we go?"

"I think that's a nice way to end our last day together."

"It's a good way to start it too."

Whitleigh smiled and bowed her head alongside her husband. Their journey began.

PSALM 91 (NKJV)

He who dwells in the secret place of the Most High
Shall abide under the shadow of the Almighty.
I will say of the LORD, *"He is* my refuge and my fortress;
My God, in Him I will trust."

Surely He shall deliver you from the snare of the fowler
And from the perilous pestilence.
He shall cover you with His feathers,
And under His wings you shall take refuge;
His truth *shall be your* shield and buckler.
You shall not be afraid of the terror by night,
Nor of the arrow *that* flies by day,
Nor of the pestilence *that* walks in darkness,
Nor of the destruction *that* lays waste at noonday.

A thousand may fall at your side,
And ten thousand at your right hand;
But it shall not come near you.
Only with your eyes shall you look,
And see the reward of the wicked.

Because you have made the LORD, *who is* my refuge,
Even the Most High, your dwelling place,
No evil shall befall you,
Nor shall any plague come near your dwelling;
For He shall give His angels charge over you,
To keep you in all your ways.
In *their* hands they shall bear you up,

Lest you dash your foot against a stone.

You shall tread upon the lion and the cobra,
The young lion and the serpent you shall trample underfoot.

"Because he has set his love upon Me, therefore I will deliver him;
I will set him on high, because he has known My name.
He shall call upon Me, and I will answer him;
I *will be* with him in trouble;
I will deliver him and honor him.
With long life I will satisfy him,
And show him My salvation."

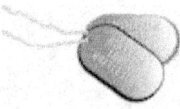

THE END

Reader's' Guide: Suggested Discussion Questions

SUGGESTED questions for a discussion group surrounding *Wedding a Warrior*.

While the characters and situations in *Wedding a Warrior* are fictional, I pray that their story parallels the truth of God's love, forgiveness, and His ability to restore in a way that sticks with the reader for a lifetime. Please search God's Word (The Bible) and prayerfully consider the questions below as you draw conclusions.

Plans are fun to make, and it's often wise to make them. However, sometimes our plans get in the way of faith. It's often difficult to know when we should let go and let God.

1: Discuss that balance of letting go and letting God versus our plans and to-do lists.

God doesn't want good for our life he wants great, however, choosing greatness often means going down a path we didn't plan. Perhaps it is dark, lonely, or painful.

2: Can you think of a time God's great plan was different from your good plan?

Fear often hinders us from following God and taking steps in faith, but we know God has not given us a spirit of fear but one of power, love, and sound mind (2 Timothy 1:7).

3: Is there something God wants or has wanted you to do, but fear got in the way?

4: Take time to pray about your answer and ask God to help remind you of the spirit of power, love, and sound mind living in you.

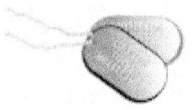

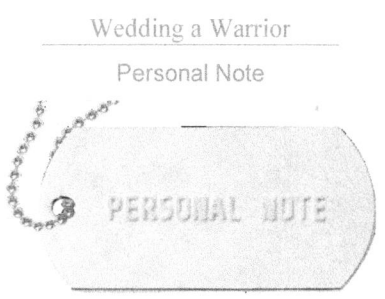

A Personal Note from Author Hannah Conway ...

Thank you for picking up this book and making the decision to read it through. There are literally millions of books out there you could've chosen, so really, it's a big deal that you picked *Wedding a Warrior*. From the bottom of my heart I thank you.

I pray *Wedding a Warrior* blessed you and encourages you not to let fear get in the way of faith. It is, however, my deepest prayer that you would know, love, and serve the God that I and my characters know, love, and serve. God doesn't want us to just believe in Him. He wants a relationship with us, and we can have that relationship with Him through His son, Jesus.

Romans 10:9 says that if we declare with our mouth that Jesus is Lord and believe God raised Him from the dead, we will be saved (Made right with God and able to be with Him after we die). I pray you've made that decision to have a relationship with God. Please feel free to connect with me through my website, mailing list, and social media sites. I'd love to hear from you and any decision you've made about following Jesus.

I can't tell you how loved and appreciated you are! Again, thank you, and I hope you enjoyed this novella! If you find yourself curious what happens to Whitleigh and Collier after this novella, don't worry, you can pick up *The Wounded Warrior's Wife*, but hold on to your seat—you're in for an adventure!

The Wounded Warrior's Wife

A Novel by

Hannah Conway

THE story of Whitleigh and Collier continues in the full length novel, *The Wounded Warrior's Wife*. Please enjoy this special excerpt.

THE last hints of sunlight poured through the modest bathroom window. The tub water, now lukewarm, retreated in slow waves across Whitleigh Cromwell's neck. Mellow tunes, defending the house from silence, drifted through the tiny tiled room. No matter the soft, easy nature of the melody, there was nothing relaxing or distracting about her *Elements of Education* textbook.

She crossed her eyes and tapped a pencil on her bottom lip before circling a long, drawn out explanation of differentiation.

How many more definitions did she have to underline? Senior-itis was kicking in two semesters too early.

Whitleigh sank lower in the tub. Studying would've been much more enjoyable with Collier home. Life in general was better with him around.

She huffed. With a wet finger, she turned the page. Waiting was the worst. Worse than reading a bound book of boredom, but that's Army life — hurry up and wait.

She couldn't complain too much though. Whitleigh closed her eyes for a moment. Her lips curved into a smile. In a manner of weeks it would be over soon. All of it. The wait, Army life — all done. Life with her husband could resume as normal. She sighed, her breath creating ripples in the water. Weeks would be no problem to pass compared to the year they'd nearly conquered, but studying seemed to be an inadequate way to pass the time.

The words in the text blurred. She squinted through the wire frames, sliding to the tip of her nose, unable to make much more sense of the paragraph.

It had been a long day. A long year.

Whitleigh snapped the book shut with a clap. Scarce patches of bubbles from the bath threatened to ruin her note page where it was balanced on the edge of the tub. She pushed the papers to safety on a footstool turned bath-time desk. An angry buzzing rang out. Whitleigh lunged from the sudsy waters, clambering for the clattering cell phone perched atop the toilet seat. A stack of textbooks fell prey to her flailing limbs.

"Whit." The line cracked and popped. "Can you hear me?"

"Sorta." She squealed and groused as soapy shampoo suds seeped into her eyes.

"Whit?"

"I'm here." She swatted the volume on the MP3 player stand

and felt around for a towel. A shirt would do the trick. Shampoo seemed as effective as pepper spray.

"Hold on." Grumbles echoed from the other end of the line. The static stopped. Whatever he did worked. "Better?"

"Loads." She laughed, her eyes still stinging as she twisted her soaking hair into a towel. "Collier, oh my gosh. I've missed you. How are you?"

The line crackled. Whitleigh threw on a robe before walking down the hall and into their bedroom. Even their phone conversation required patience with the interference and delay. She skirted around their bedroom, mindful of the books and folded laundry ready to be put away.

"I'm good, Sweets." She could almost hear the smile in his tired voice. "Just missing you."

"You counting down?" Her stomach knotted. Things were looking up.

"Yeah."

"Don't sound too excited." Whitleigh plopped on the bed and gathered a few pillows underneath her arms.

"I'm excited. Just some things, you know, going on."

Whitleigh frowned. Though Korea hadn't been a war zone in fifty years, Collier and the other soldiers spent a lot of time drilling in the field. Must be tedious work.

"Look Whit, um, I don't have much time."

"What's wrong?"

The stories that came from Korea were horrid. Soldiers cheating on their wives, drunken bar fights, prostitutes roaming the streets. She shoved those thoughts from her mind.

Not her Collier. Not ever.

"Remember that piece you heard on the news?"

"Yeah." She rolled her eyes. How could she forget? The media had about given her a heart attack. "News stations need to get their facts straight."

Collier coughed. "Anyway." He coughed again. His tone echoed hints of anxiety.

Whitleigh fidgeted with a piece of tangled, wet hair falling from the towel. Collier never hesitated with his words.

"Well, they aren't rumors anymore."

"What do you mean?"

Oh.

Wait.

What?

"War?" Whitleigh slid off the bed. "That's ridiculous. They can't send you to Iraq." She paced the room. The carpet, tan and tattered, had felt more than its share of trampling feet. "No. You've done your year in Korea." She threw up her free hand and stomped her foot. Like that would help. "They can't send you anywhere else but home."

"Whit, calm —"

"Calm down. Calm down? Really, Collier?" She clamped her jaw tight. "They have no right —"

"Whitleigh." The sharpness in his voice silenced her. Her stomach contorted, sending a wave of nausea over her body. She collapsed on the bed, fighting off tears and the urge to continue her rant.

"Listen to me, please."

How could she listen? All of the effort it took to move to Fort Carson, Colorado and transfer her college credits, ready to start her life with Collier, but then a hardship tour to South Korea interrupted. Now this?

Collier released a drawn out breath. "I wanted you to hear it from me before the crazy news people start saying stuff."

Closing her eyes, she softened her grip on the phone. He didn't deserve to be her punching bag. "I'm sorry." Whitleigh shook, drawing the pillows into her lap. "I just want you home. For good. I want us to be together."

A tear fell, and then another.

"I know, Sweets. I'll be home in two days tops."

That was good news to cling to. Whitleigh propped herself against the headboard.

"We've got two weeks of leave. We'll celebrate."

"Celebrate what? Deployment? Spending another year apart?" Whitleigh unraveled the towel from her hair and dabbed her eyes. "This isn't how I thought we'd spend our first anniversary — oceans apart."

"I know, Whit." He probably pinched the bridge of his nose. She listened as he drew in a deep breath. "Two weeks is enough time to take you on a real honeymoon."

Whitleigh held in quiet sobs. Her chin dimpled.

"I know this isn't what we planned." No it wasn't. "But it's gonna be okay." Nothing about this was okay.

His optimism made her scowl.

Collier exhaled. "Please say something."

Her bottom lip protested beneath the grip of her teeth. The tears couldn't be stopped. "I'm not sure I know what to say." Nothing from her mouth would be beneficial. Holding tongue was the most viable option.

"Listen, Sweets, I have to go. There are others in line behind me." His voice softened. "I'll... I'll see you soon."

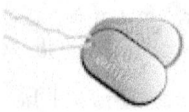

LONGEST night ever. Going to sleep wasn't an option right after receiving such devastating news. Whitleigh rolled from the bed, grumpy beyond reason. The morning news station didn't help. Twelve soldiers killed in Iraq. She turned the TV off and threw the remote on the floor. Not even a quickly brewed cup of coffee lifted her spirits. She pried the screen door open — dumb thing — and stepped down onto the broken slab of concrete.

The coffee sloshed from side to side with each grumbled movement. Her favorite hooded sweatshirt, torn and faded gray, looked as droopy as she felt. The cracked Kentucky Wildcat emblem provided no reason to discard this cozy cotton article of clothing no matter what Collier said. There were plenty of things he wore and did that she couldn't stand. Whitleigh blew a strand of hair from her face, wishing she had the energy to throw it into a ponytail.

The clinking of nails and hammers echoed through the cul-de-sac. A new subdivision was being built on base adjacent to theirs. Maybe she could convince the construction workers to do some sympathy renovations on her home.

Whitleigh sat on the cool concrete and cradled the steaming mug between her hands. Her tired, puffy, red eyes squinted in the sunlight. She sniffled and refused to let another tear fall. It was time to pull herself together. Suck it up.

Think positive. Maybe a run would help, or maybe a chocolate bar. Either of those always did a pretty good job of clearing her mind. Cookies. She was getting pretty good at baking. Maybe a good book and bubble bath would stop the aching in her chest. A tear threatened to fall, but Whitleigh blinked it away.

She took a sip, enjoying the bold flavor as it scalded her throat.

Thinking positive was harder than it seemed.

Whitleigh looked from side to side. It may not have been the wraparound porch like she'd dreamed, but there was room for a chair, sort of. Pink blooming rose bushes, flanking the sides of the porch, greeted her with a fresh floral scent. Whitleigh leaned over, prolonging an inhale. Wonderful. The new housing units didn't have these kinds of flowers.

The chilly wind pimpled her flesh with goose bumps. She crossed her arms. Spring was here, but summer needed to hurry. Like normal, the cannon blast and trumpet call sounded the beginning of a new work day on base.

She yawned and stretched. Collier hadn't spent much time in their brick matchbox, but this was their home now, broken slab of a porch and all. Maybe she could see about having the cracked siding redone and repainted. The once cheery yellow paint had faded with time, along with the grass. She might get it growing again if she could rid it of the overgrown weeds. She'd have to talk to housing about that when they opened later. Their home needed to be cozy and inviting when Collier came home in a day or so.

So much work to do. Whitleigh rubbed her brow. Too much work to do in one day.

Turning her head to the west, the corners of her mouth curved into a slight grin.

The mountains were beautiful.

Those Rockies still took her breath away and made the rolling hills of her Kentucky home look puny. Colorado Springs' pride and joy, Pike's Peak, kept a snowcap almost year around, but today it seemed spectacular, bleached even. It was stunning in the wee hours of the morning.

Whitleigh stood, drinking in the morning mountain air. So

far, Fort Carson seemed nice enough. It wasn't her old Kentucky home, that's for sure, but it was military life. Real. Hard. Each day she'd discovered it wasn't exactly what she'd romanticized.

She sighed. A tiny ant crawled along the porch step. She moved her foot to let it pass. Maybe she should skip class today. Professors were understanding people. Sometimes. Besides, there was so much other work. Whitleigh eyed the chipped paint on her fingernails.

The sound of another defiant, creaking screen door caught her attention. Whitleigh turned to wave at Mrs. Ryan, a sweet woman from across the street if you could overlook her meddling.

She sported a puffy pink robe and at least thirty hair rollers. Most of Whitleigh's neighbors were nice enough. Sort of. Though she wasn't old, this mother of five had a mother hen complex.

Mrs. Ryan hustled out into her lawn to snatch up the newspaper. She flipped a wave and scurried in Whitleigh's direction. The powdery pink fuzz balls atop her house slippers shook with each step. It wasn't the best time for a visit from Mrs. Ryan and her snooping questions.

Whitleigh forced a smile. "Good morning."

"Morning." Her lips bent into a worried glower. "I heard the news." She tucked the newspaper under her chubby arm. The pink material of the robe hid all but a portion of the paper.

Whitleigh nodded. The word that the Second Brigade Combat Team was headed to Iraq from Korea proved headline worthy. News travels fast. Surely Mom would be calling soon, along with the rest of her friends and family from back home. Maybe she should turn off her cell. No. Not at the risk of missing a call from Collier.

Mrs. Ryan's steps were careful as she neared, like the smallest movement would send Whitleigh spiraling out of control. Maybe it would.

Whitleigh sipped at her coffee and gave a half smile as Mrs. Ryan sat beside her.

"This life… these kinds of thing," Mrs. Ryan shook her head and sighed, "they can be unbearable." She picked a piece of fuzz from her robe. It fell from her fingers and floated quite a distance before landing on the sidewalk.

Whitleigh's chest throbbed. She inhaled, wishing three clicks of her heels would take her home — anywhere but here, talking about anything but this. Mrs. Ryan needed to stop prying. Maybe Whitleigh should interfere in her life. Strange how the Ryan family, being higher enlisted, still lived among privates. Strange how she never saw Mr. Ryan. Bet she wouldn't want Whitleigh asking those kinds of questions.

"You know," Mrs. Ryan scratched at her nose, "that last batch of cookies you brought over topped any of the others. All the neighbors agree." She smiled.

Whitleigh's cheeks grew hot. Talk about an insert foot in mouth moment. "Thank you." She bowed her head.

"The kids gobbled them up in minutes. I had to fight for one."

A wave of warmth washed through Whitleigh's body and dulled the ache in her chest. It was nice to be noticed. Her lips twitched upward.

"You lift our spirits with those cookies." She smacked at Whitleigh's shoulders with a hand. "And expand our waistlines." Mrs. Ryan's finely manicured nails clicked against the concrete as she giggled. "I'm glad I could squeeze a smile out of you, Whitleigh." She gave a playful nudge.

Whitleigh rubbed her hand across her forehead, grinning. "It feels good to smile."

"Bit of advice from someone who's been living this life for a while now." She put a steady hand on Whitleigh's knee. "Find reasons to smile and laugh. Keep busy. Make friends."

Easier said than done. She was trying. Trying hard to do all those things.

The coffee in her mug had grown cold. No bother. She took a sip anyway and leaned into Mrs. Ryan's hug, willing herself not to cry.

Sirens sounded in the distance, growing closer by the second.

She and Mrs. Ryan parted, standing to watch as the first police car sped by and took a squealing sharp turn onto the street behind them. An ambulance followed soon after, and then two more police cars. Blue lights ricocheted in the morning hours. Piercing sirens echoed through the housing area. If anyone were still sleeping in the neighborhood, they would be awake now.

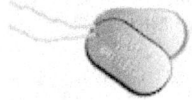

THE Military Police arrested a sobbing soldier. Whitleigh reminded herself to blink, clinging to an empty coffee mug. The story on the mid-morning news was horrific. Why had she even turned the television back on? It worsened the day, but her eyes were fixed on the screen, unable to look away. An Army wife dead, neck snapped by her husband who was on leave from Iraq. A tragic accident. Two children left without a mother, their father facing life in prison.

Whitleigh choked back tears. Her throat burned. Through the dining room blinds she could see the crime scene tape stretched across the perimeters of the house behind hers. What was this new life of hers?

She willed her fingers to click the TV off. Except for the low hum of the ceiling fan, the living room was silent.

Uncomfortable. Whitleigh sat on the couch, fingers rubbing the corduroy backing of a floral pillow. It was best to keep busy, so why couldn't she move? Collier couldn't get home soon enough.

For the most part the inside of the house was tidy. Dusting could be done in a cinch. Her textbooks and leisure reads were stacked neatly in various places around the house. Laundry could be put away in no time. Dishes were done. It wouldn't take much to run the vacuum. She was sure Collier would want to go out to eat. No need to prep a meal, though she would need to pick up his favorite sugary cereals.

A few cars started in the parking lot. Whitleigh tried not to look out toward the crime scene. Maybe she should go to class. Professors weren't always forgiving. A quick dab of mascara, and Whitleigh rushed out the door.

The Wounded Warrior's Wife is available from Olivia Kimbrell Press™ in print or ebook formats wherever fine books are sold. Visit your library or buy your own copy from your favorite bookseller today.

More Great Reads From Olivia Kimbrell Press

SEVEN women from different backgrounds and social classes come together on the common ground of a shared faith during the second World War. Each will earn a code name of a heavenly virtue. Each will risk discovery and persevere in the face of terrible odds. One will be called upon to make the ultimate sacrifice.

Best-selling Christian author, **Hallee Bridgeman**, presents a labor of love years in the making. Each story is inspired by actual events and genuine unsung heavenly heroines.

Part 1	Temperance's Trial
Part 2	Homeland's Hope
Part 3	Charity's Code
Part 4	A Parcel for Prudence
Part 5	Grace's Ground War
Part 6	Mission of Mercy
Part 7	Flight of Faith

INSPIRED by real events, these are stories of Virtues and Valor.

Find out more at www.oliviakimbrellpress.com

HANNAH CONWAY is an Army wife of more than ten years, mother of two, writer, and speaker. A Kentucky native, she and her family reside in near Fort Campbell where they are currently stationed.

Hannah holds a BA in History from the University of Colorado at Colorado Springs and has spent many years in ministry working with both youth and women's groups. She served two years as a Youth Director and one year as a Co-Coordinator of a Mothers of Preschoolers (MOPS) group.

When not writing, you'll find Hannah volunteering for community service projects, jogging (slowly), neck deep in Pinterest crafts, or browsing thrift stores. A good book, a piece of chocolate, Chai tea latte, and an outdoor setting take her captive on more occasions that she likes to admit.

The most important thing about Hannah, is that she's a follower of Christ. It's her prayer that you will come to know how much God loves you through her writings.

Author Website: www.hannahrconway.com
Facebook: www.facebook.com/authorhannahconway
Newsletter: http://tiny.cc/hannahconwaynews

www.ingramcontent.com/pod-product-compliance
Lightning Source LLC
Chambersburg PA
CBHW071925220626
47052CB00002B/458